ENDING FOREVER

NICHOLAS CONLEY

---

1.   http://StreetlightGraphics.com

Chapter 1: Contract to Die

It was six a.m., the sun was rising, and Axel Rivers had signed a contract permitting a horrendously wealthy organization to kill him—and bring him back—in exchange for money.

Cold winds whistled between concrete buildings. A bus, plastered with the pale-blue logo of Kindred Eternal Solutions, pulled up to the curb, its tires crunching through gravel in a way that sounded as tired as Axel felt. His fellow human lab rats on the sidewalk—each one's face etched with its own tale of poverty—spilled toward the bus, where an attendant checked their papers. Dozens of people had signed their lives away. And by the end of the day, Axel realized, all of them would have awoken from their first death, with six more scheduled for the week ahead.

Axel stood back from everyone else—being six feet five and built like a tank, he often pushed himself backward to make others feel more comfortable—and clutched his contract between two blistered hands. *I should walk the hell away from here*, he told himself. His foolish signature glared at him from the printed page, giving permission for his murder and resuscitation. *What kinda moron signs this?* He started to crumple the page, then stopped. *But I do need the money.*

The pay was decent enough, after all, particularly for an unemployed welder in a recession. Nothing to write home about, but it would cover a month's rent. This was the excuse he'd told his best friend, Malik, about why he'd signed up for what he'd referred to as a "sleep study." Malik had rolled his eyes at this—he always saw through

Axel's lies—but he hadn't asked questions, likely knowing that Axel wouldn't answer them. He never did.

The tangled crowd straightened into a single-file line. Axel took the last place, towering over his peers, as everyone shuffled toward the bus. Papers rustled. Some people were turned away at the door, and Axel noticed that their faces looked relieved rather than disappointed. *They must've failed the psych examinations and personal history inquiries,* he thought. *Maybe that'll get me booted, too.* The hope that this brought him, though, seemed as dim as the shards of light peeking through the cloudy sky.

Axel's phone buzzed—a reminder that his credit card payment was three months overdue. He sighed. He'd planned to use the Kindred money for rent, but at some point, he'd also have to tackle the credit cards, the personal loan, the insurance bills, the electricity, the collections bill, and all the other junk that had stacked up since The Bad Day.

Don't think about it. He closed his eyes, counted to three, then opened them.

"Papers, please," asked the attendant, a mustached man with noticeably chapped lips. Axel jolted back into reality. He held out his contract, and the attendant scanned the barcode. "Axel Rivers," the attendant said. "Thank you for your service."

Axel nodded. Part of him appreciated it when people said that. Another part of him was tired of it—tired of wondering whether people actually meant it, or if were just commending him because they felt guilty not doing so.

"When we arrive, sign in on the second floor," the attendant said. "Next!"

Axel boarded the obnoxiously short bus, ducking his head down to fit inside. *Claustrophobic. Hate it.* He hunched down into an open seat, took out his phone again, and swiped away dozens of unpaid bill reminders. Just as he was about to open his email, his photos app blasted its own reminder—"Two years ago today!" it said while displaying a photo of a little boy in a Superman costume, jumping off a couch with the world's widest grin.

Axel's heart pounded. *Aaron.*

He closed his eyes and counted to three again. *Don't think about it.* He counted to ten. *It's been a year. Don't. Think. About. It.*

Exhaling, eyes open, he pocketed his phone, thinking—not for the first time—that he should sell it online and get himself a cheap flip phone instead. Outside the window, the clouds cracked open, releasing the rainfall they'd been pregnant with all morning. Axel thought about how each individual raindrop plummeted downward—down, down, down—never knowing, perhaps, that it was headed for such a hard landing.

"Daddy," Aaron had once asked him, pointing at a puddle. *"What'll happen to that rainwater when the sun comes out?"*

"Depends," Axel had told his son. *"If the sun's hot enough? It'll evaporate, probably."*

Aaron had paused for a long time, his big hazel eyes looking remarkably concerned about this concept. *"When water evaporates, Daddy, does it... die?"*

"Nah, kid. Water never dies. It just changes."

Axel rested his head against the cool glass. He stared into the murky stream that was forming alongside the curb. *It just changes.* He stared at the contract, trembling with anxiety, and wondered if—when he died in a few hours—the Axel Rivers who came back would be the same person.

Many possible answers to this question swam through his head, but none of them brought him comfort.

"DUDE, ARE YOU FUCKING serious?" A seventeen-year-old Malik passed the burning joint. "You're joining the military... what, after graduation? That's your plan?"

The group of high schoolers laughed. Ax Rivers—back then, he didn't like using his full name—cracked a grin, though it had more to do with him being stoned than any amusement at Malik's comments. Taking the joint that was passed to him, he said, "Yeah. So?"

"It's weird. That's all," Malik said while glancing out the basement window, to make sure Tim's parents weren't coming. "No offense or anything."

Ax pulled smoke deep into his lungs. "Whatever." He stifled a cough.

"It's just not what anybody would expect from you, Ax," said Tim, their friend from History class, and the one in their friend group with the biggest house. "You're, like, a musician, dude. I thought you were gonna be the type to hit the road with your guitar, in a van or something, then hit the big leagues, be in a major band."

Ax wrapped his fingers around the neck of his guitar protectively. "I can still do that, after I get back. Can do both."

He took another hit then passed the joint to Cynthia. The group kept talking, but as the cannabis sunk into them, their voices blurred. He cared less and less what the others thought. His comfy, middle-class friends—other than Malik, his fellow foster kid—couldn't understand. They had supportive parents. Colleges to sign up for. Futures laid out for them. Families that would have their back and two-story houses with yards and garages that they could always come back to if things went wrong, with all their childhood things waiting in their childhood bedrooms.

Ax didn't have any of those luxuries. His parents had died when he was five. He had no family, no clear future, no guaranteed success. After growing up in foster care, bouncing from home to home—the latest being his current place, where his foster parents barely spoke to him and kept locks and alarms on everything from the windows to the fridge—he knew full well that the world didn't care if he failed. Nobody was in his corner. Joining the military, as much as it scared him senseless, seemed the only surefire way to build a stable future for himself.

Malik's voice broke through the smoky haze. "I'm worried you'd get killed, man," Malik said. "Aren't you scared of that?"

Ax shrugged.

"That stuff freaks me out." Malik passed the joint again. "Death, I mean. Not the physical part, but what happens after. Like, what if God is real? Or any deity. What if the universe... wherever we go, when our bodies die, what if we just have to face up to something so absurdly huge, so impossible for our dumb little brains to comprehend. Existence itself, infinity, God, whatever. I mean, what if we're just tiny fucking cogs in some goddamn huge wheel that doesn't give a shit about us, and when we die, we realize how small we really are?"

Ax had never really thought about it that way, before that day in the basement. But after hearing Malik put it that way, he never stopped thinking about it.

WHEN AXEL EXITED THE bus, the rain had stopped, much to his relief—ever since The Bad Day, rainstorms had become one of his worst triggers. He stared up at the surprisingly nondescript office building for a moment, his legs shaking like two dominos in a breeze, and then followed the crowd inside. *Turn around and march out of here, dumbass,* he thought. *No check is worth getting killed over.*

He pressed forward. The décor of the office building was elegant but artless. He followed the signs until he landed at a lobby that looked more like an emergency room—aside from the glowing blue KINDRED logo on the back wall, anyway—and was filled with rows of chairs, each one occupied, with much of the floor crowded with people as well. Most of these people, he was fairly sure, were homeless. He saw it in their clothes, their postures, and particularly the way they lowered their eyes when he faced them. Thinking about Kindred's strategy—taking advantage of the vulnerable, to create new privileges for the rich—made Axel sick, a feeling only worsened by the realization that he, too, was a vulnerable person being taken advantage of. He hated seeing himself that way.

Carefully stepping over a homeless old man sleeping on the floor—*another veteran,* he noticed—Axel approached the receptionist, who was shielded behind bulletproof glass. She was a tiny, fortysomething white woman with blond pigtails, and she flashed him a phony smile. "Hi, sir! Are you here for Kindred?"

"Yep." Axel reached behind his head, rubbing his neck. "Got this contract thing."

He slid the papers beneath the glass. She picked it up by the corner, between two fingers, as if avoiding contamination. Running down it with her spectacled eyes, she pointed to the bottom. "You left some questions blank, Mr. Rivers. Do I have your permission to get verbal answers? Kindred requires every part of this to be completed, for legal reasons."

Great. "Sure."

"Do you suffer from any underlying medical conditions?"

"Knee cartilage issues. Broke my back once, when I was in the military. Just a bad fall. Healed up, but still get pains when I lift something. Nothing else, I don't think."

"Age?"

"Thirty-four."

"Race?"

"Multiracial," he said.

She eyed him carefully. *Oh, here it comes.* He could hear her objectifying question before she even uttered it. "What are you, exactly?" she asked. "Can you be clearer?"

Axel knew there was no way to win this. Not answering led to judgment, prejudices, and more questions. Answering it did much the same. With a sigh, he finally took the tactic of overexplaining. "My mother was Cambodian. Some French, too. Father was Black. He had a white English grandparent, and some Samoan, too. Supposedly there's a little German somewhere, forget which side." He rubbed his eyes. "Clear enough for you?"

She didn't react. "Religion? Beliefs about the afterlife?"

He shrugged. "Don't know. Nothing specific."

"Hmm." She seemed annoyed by this. "Okay, well, bloodwork looks good. No criminal background. You still need to go through orientation, though. You'll be in Group 13." She passed him a slip of paper under the glass. "Now, let's see..."

A TV screen behind the woman played an antidepressant commercial, depicting a father and son on the beach, racing into the ocean together. The man held his boy up into the air, teaching him how to swim, as a muffled voice announced carefully scripted platitudes about "taking your life back" while rapidly moving subtitles listed all the potential side effects. The little boy squeezed the father's hand, and as the father smiled, Axel tensed up. *Don't think about it.* Axel closed his eyes and started counting as fear boiled within him. *Don't have an anxiety attack here. Don't do it.*

"Mr. Rivers?" the receptionist asked, and he realized that he had zoned out.

"My bad. Can you repeat that?"

"Again, for legal purposes—in the past six months, have you ever experienced suicidal thoughts, even once?"

Axel glanced back at the TV. The commercial was over. He squirmed under the receptionist's razored gaze. *You've lied your way in so far. Why stop here? You going to chicken out at the last second by telling them the truth?*

"You're going to be dying, Mr. Rivers," the receptionist said. "Over and over again. We need to know that there's no risk of you *trying* to use our program as a way to commit —"

"Don't worry," he said with a forced smile. "I'm good."

She checked a box. "Great! Welcome to Kindred."

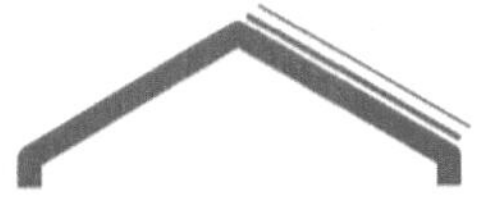

Chapter 2: Orientation

Once everyone had signed in and been reexamined, the test subjects were directed to their conference room. Axel belonged to Group 13—which meant he was directed to Room 13, as specified by the plastic tag around his neck.

Considering the flabbergasting amount of money which had been invested in Kindred Eternal Solutions, he was a bit taken aback by how shabby his surroundings were once they'd bypassed the lobby—clearly, the trillionaires and billionaires funding the operation only cared to invest in things that the outside world saw, like their logos and signage, but not when it came to the experience of the test subjects themselves. This impression only deepened when he entered the conference room, with its peeling wallpaper, cheap little folding chairs packed tightly together, and low-quality carpeting. Tall cardboard boxes functioned as makeshift trashcans.

Axel arrived into the conference room five minutes late, thanks to a bathroom break, just as the lights were dimming. A giant projector beamed onto the wall, transforming the room into a makeshift movie theater. He had no desire to squeeze between aisles into a folding chair—*nobody wants me sitting in front of them, anyway*—so he sidled into the back and poured himself a cup of coffee from a rusted carafe. He took a sip that would have been unpleasant if his body had not so desperately craved it. *Cheap. Burnt. Too hot. Whatever, at least it's coffee.*

By the time he started paying attention to the movie, he'd missed half of a speech by Kevin Tyler, the wealthiest man in the world and humankind's first trillionaire. "That's why we joined forces to start Kindred Eternal Solutions," the digital Tyler said as the camera panned back to reveal him standing next to five other white men. "So that death would no longer have to be the end."

There was an audible groan from the audience. Axel smirked. *Sure. Not the end for you people, anyway.* The men on the screen, as he knew from the internet, were the six richest people on the planet. Two of them were trillionaires. Five were billionaires. And all of them had come together to fund a scientific process where they—and anyone who could afford the insane fee—would live forever via chemical resurrection. It was a huge victory for them, and them alone, forged through experimentation on people like the ones in that conference room.

Oliver P. Harrington, the social media entrepreneur and the world's second trillionaire, took the screen. "That's why you're here today, folks," Harrington said. "When I started my first business, thanks to a small loan from my dad, my new approach to communication changed the landscape of the internet, and the newspapers called me a pioneer. And now, it's my genuine honor to say that you, too—all of you—will soon be pioneers on a whole different level. Because through these tests, we're going to conquer death. We'll ensure that death is just a comma, not a period. The end can be the beginning—"

"Yeah, *right*. Like any of us will be able to afford it," whispered a cigarette-scarred voice from Axel's side.

Axel looked down, and a thin woman wearing a black hoodie peered up at him. One blue eye glowed from behind her shaggy black bangs, emanating from her ghost-pale skin with an otherworldly quality. It took Axel a moment to realize that her eyes didn't match—one pupil was a tiny dark circle, whereas the other was dilated to the point where it almost filled up the entire iris, crowding out the blue.

"Don't you think it's bullshit?" she whispered, nudging him. "I read today that the starting price will be $100 billion. Can you believe that?" She gestured toward the wealthy men on the screen. "So yeah, these fuckers will live forever and ever, getting richer and richer. But us? Never. We're just getting paid chump change to fund their immortality."

Axel was surprised to realize he was smiling. "Yeah," he responded. "Funding it by dying for them."

"Literally."

The screen faded to black. A beaming white light shined from its center, which then opened up into an iridescent and tentacled flower unlike anything that existed on Earth. *Maybe it's from the afterlife,* Axel pondered, suddenly intrigued—and intimidated. A soft female voice reverberated from the speakers. "Welcome to Kindred Eternal Solutions, and thank you for joining us today," the voice said. More sparks of light sputtered from the flower's petals like fireflies. "You have been given the opportunity to embark on a once-in-a-lifetime adventure, which may change the nature of human society, and the human perception of death, forever."

Axel wanted a shot of something harder than coffee. *I'm going to die today. Fuck.* The whole situation didn't feel real.

"As you are now aware —" The flower's sparkling tentacles crawled across the screen like roaming snakes. The CGI was impressive, if not exactly convincing. "— this process will involve the injection of a special chemical formulation, which will cause you to enter a state that, until now, we have commonly referred to as *death*. Your heart will stop—" At this, the snakes wove into a pulsing heart, booming through the speakers. "For ten hours, and your physical body will be kept in stasis so that no degradation occurs. Meanwhile, our crack team of researchers will use bleeding-edge technology to study you, to gain new insights about death, dying, and the processes therein."

This so-called *crack team* appeared on the screen, hovering around a person whose body was stuffed inside a device that reminded Axel of an iron lung. *Jesus. What did I sign up for?* The screen then showed the same doctors standing in a line, with each doctor's academic credentials, awards, patents, and other pertinent info quickly listed beneath them. One of the doctors, a middle-aged woman with close-cropped gray hair and thin lips, looked at the camera with a strained but oddly genuine smile. A caption identified her as Dr. Kendra Carpenter.

"We're proud to work at Kindred," Dr. Carpenter said in the video. "For years, my colleagues and I have peered deep into the unknown, and we've learned more than you can possibly imagine. I understand that all of you must feel scared right now —" Her expression shifted to one of empathy, and Axel realized that she was the first person on-screen who talked or looked like a real human being. "— and to be frank, I don't blame you. This *is* scary. We've spent out whole lives running away from death. But all the greatest scientific discoveries in history have carried huge risks. Now, soon, we won't have to run away from death anymore, and it will all be thanks to you."

"She seems okay," the blue-eyed woman next to Axel whispered. "At least, compared to those other douchebags."

"Yep," Axel answered. "Hard not to prefer a human doctor to some robotic trust fund trillionaire, though."

They exchanged another smile. On the screen, a few other doctors spoke to the camera, and then the presentation cut back to the CGI animation. The glowing tendrils returned, but now, they more closely resembled vines. They looped together, growing into a giant, crystallized tree, shooting up into the stars, with what appeared to be human souls hanging from its branches like fruit.

"Once each death is complete," the orientation video said cheerfully, "we will use another injection to revive you. Just like that, you'll be back—but will you be the same, or better? That's what we're here to find out. That's why you will repeat this process, every day, for the next week."

Axel finished his coffee in a few gulps, and he dumped his cup in the makeshift cardboard-box trash bin. He looked at the hooded woman—trying to assess her unique eyes again—but she gestured toward the screen. "Check out the pretty tree," she whispered. "You can tell the powers-that-be invested some serious money in these graphics." She peered back at the trash. "Shame they couldn't spare a few bucks for any real trash cans, though."

The video had switched to an interview with a previous male test subject, who apparently had come out of the experience with big smiles and winning endorsements, probably accompanied by a larger-than-usual check from Kindred. Something seemed oddly shaky and uncomfortable about the man's expression, though, which made Axel not want to watch him too closely. Mercifully, the blue-eyed woman nudged him again, forcing him to look away from the screen. "So why are you here, tough guy?"

"Money," he whispered unconvincingly.

"Uh-huh." She poured herself a cup of coffee, adding an excessive amount of sugar but no cream. "And that's why you have the dictionary definition of existential dread written all over your face."

The orientation video ended, and the woman – seemingly realizing that her new cup of coffee was about to hit a deadline—gulped it down quickly. The lights came on. People started getting up from their chairs, yawning, and making small talk. Axel shuddered. *It's about to happen.* He looked at the exit door, then at the vein in his arm, already envisioning the needle going in. He'd used to give blood, back before The Bad Day. He'd always forced himself to watch the needle go in, to prove to himself that he could. *Just pretend that's what you're doing today. Giving blood. Not dying.*

The world spun in circles around him. He felt lightheaded. The one thing that centered him was the woman's voice. "Tell me," she said, "Are you more afraid of what might be on the other side... or that there might not *be* anything there?"

"Either one." Axel swallowed.

"Same here, I guess." She nudged him with her elbow. "Hey, good luck. My name's Brooklyn, by the way."

"Ax... Axel Rivers."

"Gotcha, Ax. Can I call you Battle-ax?" Brooklyn walked away, waving, and as her hoodie sleeve fell down, he noted that she was wearing wristbands. "See you in the afterlife, maybe. If there is one."

"Yeah," he muttered, and by the time he remembered where he was, Brooklyn had merged with the crowd of other confused test subjects. He followed her into the corridor, where armed security guards had already begun ushering people toward their death rooms.

"Rivers?" One security guard—a man even bigger than him—asked, taking his shoulder with an uncomfortable firm grip.

"Yep."

"Follow me, please. Your room is ready."

Chapter 3: The First Death of Axel Rivers

Axel had only two clear memories of his parents. One was the car crash. That memory was blurry, and he didn't like going back to it—didn't like remembering the cracked windshield, the blood smeared on the leather seats, the sounds of scraping metal, or the sight of their dead eyes as he cried out their names.

The other memory—his most treasured memory—was the weekend they stayed at the lake house.

Looking back, he wasn't sure how they'd afforded it. His parents never had much money. Maybe they'd gotten a discount, or knew the owners. Whatever the reason, vacations weren't something his family did, and he'd often figured that the reason this weekend stuck out in his memory as being so special was because it WAS special. Seeing both his parents at the same time, with nobody working and no stress, never happened.

He remembered that the weather was sunnier than it had ever seemed again. The water was cool. And to his childlike eyes, that little house on the lake felt like it touched the edge of the world.

Various pieces of the weekend rooted into his mind, perhaps out of order. He vaguely recalled Papa teaching him to swim. He remembered all of them running into the water at one point, laughing. He remembered making sandcastles, and looking back to see Mama climbing onto Papa's lap, kissing him. He remembered feeling safe when Papa hugged him, safer than he'd ever feel again.

Mostly, though, he remembered how they'd celebrated the sunset on the lake house's porch. Mama sang, and Papa played guitar, and he remembered looking at the way Papa's giant hands moved over the strings and how badly he wanted to learn how to play it. He remembered the beautiful sound of Mama's voice, singing a tune that never left him, in words he didn't understand. When she stopped singing, they had rested in front of a small chiminea on the porch—crackling with orange flames, tiny glowing sparks escaping into the stars—and he'd asked his mother what the lyrics meant.

"Just something I wrote when I was younger." She smiled, squeezing him close to her. "I used to want to be a singer. I wrote lots of songs. But that one was, most certainly, my favorite."

"But what do the words mean, Mama?"

He remembered something sad in the way she looked away from him. "I wrote it when my mother died," she said. "It's about the joys of life, but also death, and rebirth. How your memory lives on in your children. Not stuff we want to talk about right now, little one."

"But I DO want to talk about it." Ax crawled into her lap. "Can you tell me what each word means?"

She looked at Papa, who shrugged. Then, she said, "When you're a little older, and you learn how to speak Khmer, you will know all the words to my song."

"What's the name of it?"

"The title." She stared out into the water, then decided to answer him. "I called it 'Ending Forever,' when I first wrote it."

At this point, the memories became a bit fuzzier. There was more singing. Laughing. They played a game. Then at some point, Papa lifted Ax onto his shoulders, pointed out into the lake, and when Ax said that they were on the edge of the world, Papa said, "No, son. That out there, on the horizon." He pointed. "It's the beginning of the world. And it's all yours to explore. To dream. Remember that."

At that, Ax went quiet. Then, he'd said, "I don't want this day to end. It's been the best day ever."

"It will end," Mama said. "Everything does."

"I don't want it to."

Papa put him back down on his feet, and he hugged Mama's legs. "You can't control that," she said, nestling her fingers in his hair. "But if you focus, if you try really hard, you can make sure you remember this day, and that way, in a sense, it WILL last forever." She pointed at the moon. "Take in all of the tiny details. Each one. First, focus on the moon. Look at the way it glows. See the little imprints on its surface. Tell yourself, Ax, 'I will remember that,' and you will."

Ax pointed at the moon. "I will remember that."

"Now." She pointed at a distant bonfire on the beach, in front of another lake house. "Remember the light of that fire, in the distance, and say—"

"I will remember that." Ax giggled.

Papa and Mama smiled at one another. Then, she pulled Ax in for a hug. "Remember what it feels like when I hold you close. How warm it is. How loved you feel. Remember how much your Mama and Papa love you."

"I will remember that!" He jumped.

"Good. Now look at the stars. Look at how many of them there are. Space—it's so enormous, isn't it? And say —"

"I will remember that."

They all sat down together, and they looked at the water. "When you remember these moments, they last forever," Mama said. "You promise to remember this?"

Ax grinned. "I promise."

AXEL HAD ALWAYS HATED going to the doctor's office. He'd hated being examined in general. His whole life, people had always stared at him, inspected him, asked personal questions, and made him feel as if he were not good enough. There were one or two places he'd ever felt comfortable putting his truest self out there. The first one had been up on a stage, behind a guitar... before he'd lost the motivation to play. The second was with his wife Shoshana, back when things were happy, back in the years before the heavy gates to his thoughts—the ones she'd worked so hard to unlock—had suddenly slammed shut, without warning. *I'm sorry, Shoshana. It's my fault.*

A light shined in Axel's eyes, breaking through his attempt at distracting himself and forcing him to remember that he was cold, half-naked, and spread out on an operating table, about to have his dead body hooked up to wires, slid into a mechanical coffin, and studied. The attendant in front of him scrawled something into a pad, and said, "Dr. Carpenter will be here with you in a few minutes."

The attendant left the room, leaving Axel alone in his existential terror. *I shouldn't be here. I need to get out. Out. Now. Except I need the paycheck...* He stopped his train of thought. *Don't lie to yourself, dumbass. You know the real reason you're here. Because you want to see them. Everyone you've lost. And maybe you will—maybe you can talk to them, apologize, find a purpose again. Maybe you should be excited.* It was hard to be excited, though, when nobody would confirm to him that anything—much less his dead loved ones—waited on the other side.

The door opened, and a small group of doctors entered, led by Dr. Kendra Carpenter – the same Dr. Carpenter from the video, with her short gray hair. They made eye contact, and Axel felt an odd sense of excitement, almost as if he were meeting a celebrity.

Dr. Carpenter smiled wanly, as if reading his mind. "Hello, Mr. Rivers," she said. "You don't look nervous at all."

Despite his screeching anxiety, Axel smirked. *Sarcasm sure does do a hell of a job diffusing tension.* "Yeah," he said, "Just chilling in here. Totally cool."

"I'll bet," Dr. Carpenter smiled, and then studied the computer screen for a minute. "Well, let's get this started." She snapped on a pair of rubber gloves. Meanwhile, the group of doctors checked his vitals again. Axel's lungs couldn't take in air. His vision blurred. He couldn't think straight. *Stay calm. Stay calm. Stay—*

"Mr. Rivers?" Dr. Carpenter asked from beneath a surgical mask. "Axel?"

Axel shook his head. "Yeah?"

"We're going to begin." A pause. Axel saw her clutching a long needle full of liquid death. "Is there anything we can get you first?"

His heart pounded in his chest. *I can't do this.* He tried to sit upright, but he was strapped down. His heart raced. "No." He gulped. "No, I can't. I can't be here." *I don't want to die.* "Please get me out. I…" He exhaled, trying to calm himself down. "Please, Dr. Carpenter, can you just tell me if people see something when they die? That something exists. Just tell me that and I'll feel okay."

"Sorry, Axel. We're not at liberty to discuss—"

"Do they?"

"Relax, Axel," Dr. Carpenter said, very clearly repeating something she'd said a million times before. "It's going to be okay." And before he could resist her, a sharp pain jutted into his arm, breaking open the vein. *Shit.* His breathing slowed. *No. I can't do this.* His heart rate slowed with his breathing. "Please. I don't want to die." He gasped for air as it left his lungs. "Please. Please."

Dr. Carpenter held his hand. He clung to her with all the fading strength he had left. "It's going to be okay, Axel," Dr. Carpenter said with a gentleness that was almost reassuring. "I promise, we'll bring you back to life. It will go by in the blink of an eye. Just try to calm down and it will…"

Her voice faded out. A red light blinked in his eyes, blinding him, forcing itself to be the last thing he ever saw in his first life. His body slackened. He couldn't feel his fingers or toes. Coldness prickled through him. *So… so heavy. Heavy. Slowwwww…* He stared into the light, but his vision was darkening quickly. His heart slowed down, from a frenetic locomotive into an increasingly irregular thump.

Everything disappeared. The red light was gone. Axel heard his heart thud to a stop... and then, he heard nothing at all.

NOTHINGNESS. EMPTINESS. The void.

Gone.

Nothingness surrounds Axel, fills him, and erases everything that is left. *It's so dark,* he thinks, but he realizes that this isn't true, because darkness requires light. Here, there is no light, nor dark. No contrasts. No colors. No sounds. No smells. He is dying. *No.* He is dead.

He tries to announce his death, but he has no mouth. Screaming is an impossibility. His larynx is a memory, and then even the physical memory of it soon disappears. He tries to move. There is no movement. There is no Axel. Axel Rivers does not exist. Axel Rivers never existed. His life was a lie imprinted on an uncaring universe, wiped away by the fate that awaits all such lies. Now, he has rejoined the void, where nothing ever was and never will be.

Oh god. No. This can't be it.

There is nothing. Nothing at all. The person-who-was-Axel feels nothing. There is nothing. No afterlife. Just perpetual nothingness, swallowing everything that once was, consuming it, until nothing remains where nothing once was. Nothing remains in Axel's place. No mind. No thoughts. No consciousness. No soul.

Wait. I hear something. Please, let that be... is it water?

Yes, he hears water.

Please be real. Then, water bubbles into his lungs. He is drowning. He pushes his limbs outward—feeling limbs of some sort, though he's scared to question whether they're the same ones he had on Earth—and finds that he's trapped in a gelatinous bubble. His fingers press against something cold and wet. Somewhere in the nothingness, he hears a humming sound.

Something. There is something.

Light shimmers in a place he can feel but not see. It's not the comforting light he would have hoped for—it stings. Burns. Sizzles. *That light shouldn't be here. It feels wrong. Forced.* A high-pitched whine emits from the light, breaking through the humming. It's painful to hear. It grows louder and louder. *It sounds wrong.* He doesn't want to come close to this light, but it draws him in, and there is a dark spot in its center. There, he finds a human figure standing before him, clad in a dark, hooded robe. One of its hands is mangled. Its face is hidden in the shadows. Axel reaches for the apparition, craving contact, and when he touches its robe, he hears words—no, he *feels* words, burning themselves into his fingertips, like tiny open flames, and they say...

"The Stranger is waiting for you."

A FLASHING RED LIGHT appeared. Shapes. Sounds. Mechanical beeping noises. Velcro straps. Then Axel saw a nametag floating over him, with a photograph of a smiling woman named Dr. Kendra Carpenter. *The lead doctor.* His heartbeat pounded in his ears. *My heart. I'm... I'm...* He patted himself in disbelief, no longer strapped down. *Is this real?* He had gooseflesh.

Dr. Carpenter touched his arm. "Axel, you're alive. It's okay."

Axel shot bolt upright, gasping for air. His body felt like he was trapped in a freezer. He could barely see—colors were running down his vision and blending together like streaks of melting paint. Finally, everything reformed, and he perceived that he was sitting in the same room he'd died in, with a group of faceless doctors standing around him, holding clipboards and medical instruments.

"Axel, focus on the sound of my voice. Center yourself," Dr. Carpenter said from behind her mask. "How many fingers am I holding up?"

Blurry little appendages wobbled back and forth. They became fingers. "T-Two," he gasped.

"Welcome back." Dr. Carpenter nodded. "The first time can be a little alarming for new patients. Are you all right?"

With a slack jaw, Axel stared at her. She didn't seem real. Nothing did. His back dripped with sweat. Tears ran down his cheeks, and when he tried to speak, only sobs sputtered out. "There's no one there." He swallowed. "Nothing, but... but..." *Nothing but the Stranger. Whatever the hell that was.*

The doctors took his vitals one more time. He said nothing more. And at that moment, surrounded by people, Axel Rivers had never felt so alone.

Chapter 4: Resurrection Fatigue

Axel never forgot the first time he saw someone—other than his parents, that is—die in front of him.

It had happened overseas. The air was thick with dust and gunfire. He had pulled the trigger on the man standing before him. Hours later, thinking back on the finer details, he realized that his bullets hadn't been the ones to connect—rather, it was his friend beside him who had shot the man, while Axel had simply shot up the dirt—but at the time, all he could focus on was that someone had been standing before him, and that person had dropped lifeless to the ground. Alive, and then not alive. And while he'd always expected to feel something about a person dying in front of him, whether guilt or anger or frustration at a society that had pushed him to kill another person, he'd instead felt something far more selfish—and that was relief. Relief that he was alive. Relief that the other man wasn't.

He remembered running past the dead man's body, but stealing one look backward, and looking into his dead eyes on his dead face. The man looked so normal. He looked so... similar to Axel. Like Axel, he wore body armor and wielded weaponry. Axel realized just how easily, in the blink of an eye, that man's bullets might've met Axel's body instead, and he realized that in the terrifying frenzy of the world around him—in the messiness of everything he'd launched himself into—the notion of whether he was dead, or the other man was dead, meant very little to anyone else except the two of them. The universe didn't care. It didn't matter. None of it mattered. The war that had forced one of them to die, while the other lived, didn't matter either, devised as it was by powerful and privileged men, over moneyed interests, while regular people like him spilled their blood over the dirt.

All that mattered was someone was dead, and that the dead person—whoever they might be—would never hug a loved one, ever again. Axel would never know the man's name. And if he had died, that man would've never known his name either.

BY THE TIME AXEL WENT backed outside, the sun had clearly lasted a few minutes past its expiration date. All the milky leftover light was rapidly darkening beneath the clouds. Rain drizzled over the parking lot.

Only forty-five minutes had passed since Axel's resurrection, but as he stood outside the dull corporate building that had stolen his first life, it felt like he'd been awake for hours. He'd still barely interacted with the world—every breath, every movement, every sensation felt surreal and alien, to the point where he wanted to cut a hole in reality and crawl into it so he wouldn't feel anything again. *Except the Stranger would be there. And I don't want to ever see that again.* He hadn't talked to anyone, and his fellow test subjects weren't talking to each other either. The air was silent other than the pitter-pattering of rain and the distant sound of an ambulance a few miles away. *Someone else meeting the Stranger.*

Death wasn't what he'd expected. He hadn't gone in with any clear expectations or beliefs, either. Somehow, that made the emptiness he'd found—and the utter lack of his own ability to comprehend it—even worse. *I at least expected to see a light... well, a nice light. Something that felt like a higher power. Something with answers. Not that horrible, artificial-feeling light, whatever it was. I wanted to talk to the people I loved who died before me. Maybe even to see, you know, my life flashing before my eyes. Instead, it just felt like drowning.*

Rain speckled his shoulders. He shivered, trying not to let the weather force him back into the memories of The Bad Day, which might be the only thing still worse than dying. *Aaron, are you in that terrible void?* This thought made him feel sick. When Aaron had died, he'd often only been able to fall sleep at night by imagining his son in a happier, better place. Sometimes, he'd even envisioned Aaron's heaven as being a sloping green field with a perfect blue sky, where the little boy giggled as he chased after a magical, friendly dragon. *He always loved dragons. Drew them all the time.* Now, Axel realized, even that coping mechanism was ruined. *Because there's no field. No friendly goddamn dragon. Just the Stranger.*

Axel closed his eyes, counted to three, and tried to remember Aaron's face, to hear his voice, and to feel him scampering up onto him, asking to be swung around in circles. It took a moment, but the images came back. With every passing week, though, these memories became fuzzier and fuzzier. He dreaded the day he'd require photographs to remember the expressions of his own son.

"Hey, Battle-ax." It was Brooklyn, the woman from orientation. Her uneven eyes—one small, one large, one black, one blue—were naked with fear. He didn't have to ask why. "Any chance you've got a light?"

Axel shook his head.

"Nobody smokes anymore," she muttered, pocketing her cigarette. "I guess I should probably quit these things, too, now that we know how much death sucks, huh?" She crossed her arms.

Axel sighed. "Guess so."

He didn't know what else to say. Neither did she. However, when Brooklyn leaned into Axel's body—her bony shape taking comfort in his chest—he was surprised by how quickly he hugged her close to him. They were complete strangers, yet the biological need for human connection, after such a bizarre trauma, was overwhelming. After a few moments, she pulled away but continued holding his arm. "Hey, I know I'm just some nutcase to you—"

"Nah, I don't think you're a nutcase."

"Whatever. I mean, we don't know each other. But after going through that... look, whatever *that* was, it was one hundred percent horrendous. So, maybe, do you want to... I don't know, grab a drink together? There's a cheap new bar about ten minutes from here, walking distance, called Beelze Brews. We could check it out, if you want."

Axel stared blankly into her eyes, taking far too long to realize that he needed to respond. "I can't. Sorry. I'm married." Then he touched his naked ring finger, and the emptiness of it sent chills down his spine.

Brooklyn looked confused. "*Are* you?" She let go of his arm.

Axel looked at his bare finger again. "Well, I was." He dug his hands into his pockets. *Was. Past tense. Hate that. God, Shoshana, I miss you.* The bus pulled up to the curb, and Axel stared fixedly at it. "I should go."

"Don't worry about it, I guess." Her drapery of black hair swung toward the bus. "My fault for making assumptions."

"Brooklyn, you're fine. No worries." Axel paused, measuring his words. "Can I ask you something unrelated?" She stared at him, and before she could change her mind, he spat out his question. "When you were dead, did you see something called the Stranger?"

"I think you know." She smiled in a manner that could only be called despairing, and she clutched herself tightly. "See ya later, Battle-ax."

She hurried to the bus. Axel watched her go, letting her words sink in. The world looked different to him now—it looked temporary, flimsy, in a way it never had. *Because it is flimsy. Life is flimsy.* He watched each person getting onto the bus, Brooklyn included. *All of them are temporary, too.*

Then, he tried to visualize Aaron's smile, and for a moment in time—a few seconds that felt like a few hours—he couldn't remember what his son's happiness had ever looked like. All he remembered was the last time he'd looked into the boy's pleading eyes, in their last moments together, and he'd told him that he couldn't go with him.

If Brooklyn saw the Stranger when she died, so did Aaron. So does everyone. Just like I'll see it again tomorrow. When I die a second time.

"I'm sorry, Aaron," he whispered.

Chapter 5: Stranded in Real Life

That night, a thunderstorm broke out. The bus rumbled through dark streets, and whenever the coastline came into view, Axel gripped tightly onto his legs, trying not to think of The Bad Day. He felt as if the skeletal hand of his son was reaching up from the grave and clenching his heart, squeezing tighter with every passing minute.

Aaron isn't actually reaching for me, though. He's in the void now. Drowning forever.

While Axel hadn't mouthed a word since the bus departed from Kindred, some of the other passengers had gotten to talking, albeit in hushed voices. He didn't know if anybody was trading death stories—most likely not, he thought, as the details were still too raw and unnerving—but the two women sitting across from him were connecting on other shared experienced.

"That's a cool tattoo," one woman said, as the other revealed her bicep. "Is it... a tree?"

"Yggdrasil, the sacred world tree. Norse mythology," the other woman replied. "Each of the nine realms hangs from its branches. I got this in my twenties, after studying my Viking ancestry..."

Axel stared at the tattoo and sighed. The conversation between the women rang with familiarity, bringing back memories that had once sent him soaring but now only weighed his heart down further. *Shoshana, I miss you so much.*

ON THE THURSDAY NIGHT of Axel's twenty-fourth birthday, his band, the Iron Octopus Skeletons, went onstage at Murphy's Irish Pub. Axel played guitar. Malik did vocals. Joe was on bass. After two drummers had quit, Julio had taken over about six months prior, and the band had finally seemed complete. That night, the world felt right. Music blasted in their ears. The crowd cheered and danced. He and the guys absorbed every flicker of one another's energy, and when Malik summoned the crowd to sing "Happy Birthday"—over a hundred people, all singing a silly song, dedicated to Axel—he almost couldn't believe how comfortable he felt in his own skin.

The last few years had been hard. His time in the military had left its scars—he rarely slept a full night anymore—and while the GI Bill paid for his education, the sense of disconnect he'd always felt with others had only worsened since coming back stateside. For about six months, he'd dived heavily into trying different drugs, gone broke, and focused on music for the year following that. His guitar had proven a better outlet, but he still barely felt alive: His little studio apartment contained no furniture, and rarely had visitors. At that moment onstage, though, none of it mattered. He felt seen. He felt connected to the world, to life, and to himself.

The moment ended, of course, as all moments do. After the band finished its set, the members dispersed across the bar, and everything normalized. Malik went to go flirt with the guys on the porch, as he always did. Julio shot for the pool tables. Axel, as usual, went right to the bar to get the free drink that Murphy's offered whenever they played. That much was normal. Playing at Murphy's was normal. What wasn't normal—and what changed everything, forever—was the voice that Axel heard from the other side of the bar.

"Happy birthday," she said.

The bartender was tall, wiry, with freckled white cheeks and curly black hair tumbling down her equally black tank top. Her glasses were oversized for her small round face, and so was her denim jacket. Her movements were jittery, but her smile was confident enough to leave Axel feeling disarmed. He felt as if he recognized her—even though he knew he didn't—and when he tried to respond, all he could say was, "Thanks."

She passed him a tall glass of beer. "You got it." She adjusted her glasses, and something about her gave Axel the sense that she was a bookworm, or at least an honor roll college student. Not the type of person who usually served drinks at Murphy's. "You new?" he asked.

"Is it that obvious? Yikes." She clenched her teeth, humorously. "Yeah. Sorry if I messed something up."

"Nah, you're doing great. What's your name?"

"Shoshana."

"I'm Axel."

"I think everybody in the bar knows that. I mean, since we sang your name." She laughed, and so did he.

He eyed the tattoo running subtly up the side of her neck, almost hidden beneath her curls—a geometric sequence of circles, linked by lines, placed into a fascinating diagram. "That's a great design." He pointed. "What does it mean?"

"Oh, this?" She touched her throat. "It's the Tree of Life. Kabbalah... you know, Jewish mysticism. The circles are the ten Sefirot, the lines are the twenty-two pathways... it represents a sequence of emanations from the divine source, different aspects of the eternal. Ein Sof. The continual process of creation... and yes, I'm Jewish, if my name doesn't give it away."

"I thought I read somewhere that Jewish people didn't get tattoos."

She laughed again, rolling her eyes exaggeratedly. "It's... a debate, that's for sure. My mom wasn't happy about it. Lots of us do get them, though, particularly younger Jewish people. I even have a friend at the local synagogue with a dragon tattooed on his shoulder. Lots of others don't, though, and definitely not Orthodox—oops, hold on." She rushed over to serve a waiting customer. Axel drank his beer, waited, and right as he was about to give up on her coming back, she returned. "So, Axel..." she started, then—eyes flickering—stopped. "Sorry, am I talking too much? You probably have other people that you want to —"

"You're good," he said, trying to hide just how interested he was. "I like talking to you."

"Same," she said. "Not sure why." Catching herself, she added, "No offense. I didn't mean it in a bad way."

He chuckled. "None taken."

She poured a drink for herself, which caught Axel off-guard – she was more rebellious than he'd thought. "Okay, cool," she said. "So can I ask what first got you into playing music?"

Normally, Axel didn't answer this sort of question. He didn't like people prying inward—whenever they did, he tended to learn things about himself that he didn't like. On his birthday, though, while talking to this strange new bartender, he felt more open than usual. "Music reminds me of my parents."

"Are you close to them?"

"Well, not really. They're dead."

"I'm so sorry, I didn't mean to —"

"Nah, it's okay. They died, and I don't remember much, or have any siblings to talk to about it, but I know my mom loved to sing. Dad played guitar. Playing music reminds me of them, makes me feel like I have roots. A history." He took a drink, focused on his memory of the lake house for a moment, then smiled. "Normally, I hate birthdays, honestly. Growing up, other kids got parties, phone calls, all that, and I hate whining about it... I mean, there are other people who've got harder lives than I do. But birthdays in the past just reminded me that they were gone. And playing music, to me, it keeps them alive. Plus, I have a hard time talking to people, but when I open myself up with a guitar..." He gestured at the stage. "I don't know. Feels more natural. More real."

"That's beautiful," Shoshana said, touching his hand. And somehow—despite the dozens of people surrounding them, the clinks of glasses, and the background whine of the next band testing out an electric guitar—in that moment, they felt like the only two people in the room. "Lis-

ten, Axel, I lost my mom last year," she said. "My dad a year before that. It's so hard without them here, being an adult orphan..."

"I'm sorry," Axel said.

She exhaled. "Appreciate that." She peered up inquisitively. "Not to sidetrack, but what'd you think happens after death? I used to enjoy thinking about it, reading about it, having philosophical conversations, but ever since my parents died, it just freaks me out. I can't stop wondering."

"Stresses me out, too." He took a drink. "Hate the thought that there might be nothing. That we're just dust."

"Cosmic dust, though. Am I right?" She laughed. "When I need to feel better..." she paused, looking again to make sure there were no customers waiting for her. "I think back to this physics book I read in college, which talked about the Law of Conservation of Energy. And that law... well, if I remember correctly, it says that 'Energy cannot be created or destroyed.' So if we're made of energy, you know, that energy has to go somewhere when we die. It never actually goes away. So we never totally cease to exist, right? Our energy must just get redistributed... sorry, am I making sense?"

Axel smiled. "Perfect sense. I like that."

She touched his hand for a second, nervously realized what she was doing, and jerked away. "Glad I'm not boring you."

"Nah. Physics... so you're in school?" He cocked his head to the side. "Bet you're a physics major, actually. You seem smart as hell."

She blushed. "After my parents died... well, I dropped out, actually. That's why I'm here bartending, to be honest, because I don't even know what I want out of life anymore. But I feel stupid complaining, because look at you—at least I had my parents, growing up. I still have my sister, even if she lives all the way in goddamn Florida these days. I can't imagine if I'd had to grow up without my family at all, like you did. It must've been so hard."

"Sure was." He looked down into his drink.

"But listen." She held his hand. "Hearing you now, seeing you up on that stage playing your heart out, I can tell you—they'd be so proud of you. Your parents, I mean."

He was surprised to feel tears in his eyes. "You think?"

"Yeah." Shoshana nodded, and he saw that she'd also teared up. She squeezed his hand then let go. "Sheesh. Sorry, I'm probably rattling your ears off. Sorry."

"No, just apologizing too much." Axel grinned, and she laughed. Wiping his eyes, he raised his glass. "Well, hey, cheers to finding another adult orphan. Being less alone, if just for a minute."

"Cheers," she said, and they clinked glasses.

"CHEERS," AXEL WHISPERED to himself.

The rain had died down. As Axel mounted the concrete stairs at the front of his brick apartment building, each step felt heavier than the last. His knees were spongy. His stomach felt sick. *The Stranger, whatever the hell it is, is waiting for me. There was no deity, no joy, just that weird... whatever it was. And there's no way to get away from it. Even if I quit this Kindred shit, I have to die eventually. That's what waits at the end... if it even ends, after that. What if that nightmare just goes on for eternity? Fuck. What does eternity even feel like?*

He paused, breathed deeply, and waited for his heart to slow down. *Eternity. No. Focus on this minute. Just the right here and right now of it all.* Finally, he walked inside, past the row of mailboxes, and he unlocked his apartment. The lights were on. Dinner was left on the table, covered in plastic wrap. Axel smiled, thinking—for a painfully fleeting moment—that Shoshana had made dinner. *Except she wouldn't do that. Couldn't do that.* He buried his naked ring finger in his pocket, and he stepped inside. Unwrapping the plastic from around the plate, he found a medium-rare steak and sweet potato fries.

A toilet flushed down the hall, startling him. Malik emerged, grinned, and clapped Axel on the shoulder. "Hey, buddy," Malik said. "Made a bunch of these at the restaurant tonight. Figured you'd love to have one, so I brought it here when I got out and made it right in your kitchen. I feel lucky I even found a frying pan, considering how unorganized you keep all those cabinets." He yawned. "Didn't expect you to take so long to get here, though."

"Thanks," Axel muttered. Realizing he might be sounding dismissive—and not meaning to be—he added, "Seriously. Appreciate it."

"Bon appetit, man. Sit down and enjoy the deliciousness." He pulled out a chair and all but pushed Axel into it. "I want to hear about this weird-ass clinical trial you're getting paid for." He sat across from him. "A sleep study, right?"

"Yeah."

"Oh, yesssssss," Malik said in a rattling monster voice. "A lab rat you've become, oh yessss..." With a laugh, he checked the time on his phone. "Tell me about it, dude. I haven't got all night."

Axel stared at the steak. It looked terrific, but his appetite felt as dead as he had been a few hours ago. "Sorry, can't talk about it. Signed an NDA."

"Oh, c'mon," Malik said. "I'm not gonna tell anybody."

"Sorry." Axel took a bite. *Damn good. He's always been an amazing chef.* "This is great, though. Best steak I've had in years." Malik nodded, appreciating this, but Axel could tell how desperately his friend wanted to hear the details.

"You've gotta talk to me more," Malik said, trying to mask his irritation with a smile. "We're the two foster kids who stayed connected, man. Just like you, I haven't got parents. No uncles or aunts, no siblings. Nothing but you in my history book to prove that I even *have* a history."

"Don't guilt trip me," Axel said. "Please, I just—"

"Just won't talk?" Malik replied. "Listen, I've got things I want to talk to you about, too. Nothing huge, just… life stuff, you know? Sometimes I want to tell you how great things are going with me and Liam, or to bust out complaints about a bad day at work. But you never text me back. And if we don't talk about shit, more time passes, and we just drift further and further away from —"

"You have a partner to vent to. A life. Friends. I don't have that," Axel said, and seeing the pain in his friend's eyes, he immediately wished he hadn't. "Sorry," he whispered.

"It's cool," Malik sighed. "You're not wrong. My bad. Maybe I'm pushing you too hard. I can't imagine having to go through the stuff you did."

Axel stared into Malik's softened eyes. Ever since The Bad Day, the distance between him and Malik—and Malik's determined efforts to close that distance—had only grown more noticeable. When Axel stopped answering phone calls, Malik started coming over unannounced. When Axel didn't talk much, Malik bought him drinks. Sometimes he'd drop by in the dead of night, claiming that he was on the way back from seeing his boyfriend, Liam, but Axel knew the truth—he knew that Malik was scared of not coming by, of not being there to stop him if something bad happened. And the fact that Axel knew this—the fact that he knew his inability to communicate about the black hole inside him and his increasing avoidance of all socialization, made him a terrible friend—only made him feel worse every time they interacted.

"Hey, let me change the subject." Malik drummed the table. "You hear that Murphy's is doing open-mic nights again?"

Axel took another bite of steak. He eyed his acoustic guitar, in the corner of the room, and felt horrible for having not touched it in so long. Just a few months ago, he'd even listed it for sale online, only to yank the ad down minutes later in shame. "I heard."

"It's pretty cool," Malik continued. "We should go. I mean, I know we don't have a band anymore or anything, but man, the world is missing out on your artistic talent! Maybe next week? Or if that's too soon, the week after."

"No." Axel shook his head. "I can't." *It's just another thing I've failed at*, he thought, but didn't have the confidence to say aloud. *Just like I failed at being a father. Or a friend. Or a husband.*

Malik sighed. "All right, buddy. You look dead tired. I'm going to crash at Liam's tonight, anyway, so I'll let you get some rest. We need to talk tomorrow, though, got it? Call me. Text me. Or bust out a pen and write me some damn snail mail. Whatever. As long as I get to hear from you, okay?"

Axel tried to smile. "Or you'll just break in again, right?"

"That's what friends are for." And with that, Malik grabbed his coat, grabbed his keys from the counter, and opened the door. Then Malik stopped. "I can't just leave," he said quietly. "Ax, I've gotta ask you something."

Axel shut his eyes. *Damn it.*

"The gun safe..." Malik turned around. "I know I shouldn't be, like, snooping through your house. It's a creepy thing to do to your friend, I know. But your bedroom door was open, and I saw that... I saw, Axel. The gun was missing."

"It's on the porch." Axel said, his heart racing. "Forgot it out there last night. Didn't think about it in the morning. Was in a rush."

"But... you had it *out.*" Malik stared intently.

"Cleaning it." He clenched his teeth. *Don't ask me. Please don't make me lie to you.*

"Were you?"

Axel swallowed. *No, I was putting it in my mouth. Just to see what it felt like. That's what I was doing, Malik. Just like I was three months ago, on that other night you came in unannounced.* "Yeah. Cleaning it," Axel said, finally.

Malik nodded to himself. Axel knew Malik didn't believe him, which also meant Malik was letting himself be lied to. "Good. Don't you dare do something stupid, okay?"

"I won't," Axel said.

AFTER MALIK LEFT, AXEL sat in silence—not eating—for nearly thirty minutes. He didn't want to go to the bedroom. The submission of sleep felt too similar to death. *A mini-death. That's what it's like. Maybe sleeping takes you to a place halfway there. Maybe the Stranger is there, too.*

After spending another ten minutes debating whether to pick up his guitar or not, he instead decided to do dishes. He turned on the faucet, squeezed some soap onto the sponge, and began scrubbing the pans. Somehow, the feeling of washing the dishes was relieving. It brought back the past. He recalled a Friday night, long ago, when he'd done the dishes and listened to Aaron and Shoshana playing cards at the table, the room lit only by the gentle flames of her twin Shabbat candles. "*Uno!*" Aaron yelled as Shoshana laughed, and Axel remembered rushing through the rest of the dishes so he could join the game faster.

That life is gone. All of it. He turned off the tap. The door creaked open. *Damn it. Malik always forgets to push it all the way closed.*

A cold hand rubbed the back of his neck, and a soft, ethereal female voice emanated from beside him.

"Hey, Axel," Shoshana said, causing Axel to jump from his skin. "Are you okay?"

Chapter 6: Ghosts of the Past

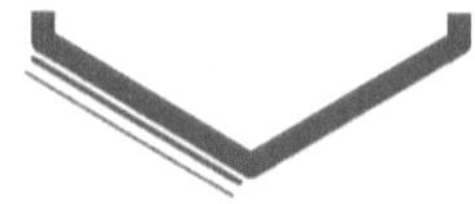

Axel slowly pieced together each of Shoshana's features, in disbelief at the fact that she was there. He counted her multiple earrings. He traced the Kabbalah tattoo on her neck, and he followed her black curls as they bounced down her neck. He followed the curve of her hips and the way her black-fingernailed hands suddenly dug into the pockets of her green bathrobe, as if hiding from him. *I got her that robe. Thrift store find.* He shook his head. *She's here. In the kitchen. It's …*

"Uh, Axel?" she said.

During Axel's confused silence, Shoshana's own gaze was sharply focused on him, with the fixed concentration that—during many occasions in the years they'd spent together—had often made others laugh uncomfortably, fidget, or look away from her. "You're here," Axel whispered. "I can't believe it."

"Just checking that you're okay. Don't read too much into it." Her eyes flicked to the pile of dishes then back to him. "I suppose I'm just bothered by the fact that you signed up for Kindred's death trial. I mean... Axel, I'm sorry, but that doesn't *sound* like someone who is doing okay."

He rubbed his eyes. *How the hell is she here?* He looked up, and she'd moved closer. "I'm fine," he said, noticing that she still wore her wedding band. He tried not to tear up. *Sick of doing that.* "As long as you're here, Shosh, it makes everything okay."

"I'm not truly here, Axel," she said as the glare of the overhead light hit her glasses, and her eyes disappeared behind the lenses.

Axel reached forward to take her into his arms—to breathe in her scent, to ease the pain that had consumed him for the last year—but as he approached, a headache split his skull open.

He clenched his teeth and buckled forward. His eardrums were pierced by the same high-pitched whining noise he'd heard when he was dead. *Not now. Please, not now.* Slowly, as he struggled to open his eyes, the whine was drowned out by the ambient noise of a tidal wave crashing against the shore. By the time he regained his senses, there was nothing—no wave, no water, no whine, no wife.

"Shoshana?" She wasn't there. She hadn't been there.

Oh no. He stumbled to the living room. *Shit, I'm hallucinating. This isn't good.* He buried his head in his hands as the black pit inside him re-opened—deeper, darker than before—and all the temporary feelings of hope he'd embraced at the miraculous sight of his wife collapsed within it. *You know damn well that she wasn't here.* He realized this, as much as he wanted to deny it. *She couldn't have been here, because...*

Because she's dead. He repeated this to himself, to drill it in. *Shoshana's dead. Aaron's dead. They died together, without you, and it's your damn fault.*

He got up and turned off the lights, wanting to hide away from the world as well as from whatever unperceivable dangers lay outside its barriers. Even with the lights off, though, the streetlight outside the window cast a yellow glow across the horrendously messy, cluttered living room. The coffee table was covered in unpaid bills so old they'd probably multiplied by now. The carpet hadn't been vacuumed in months. And as Axel sat within the shadows, pain drilling into his temples, he tried to figure out if he'd completely snapped.

I can't believe I just hallucinated her. I've never done that. He tried to deal with this information as practically as he could, but his pounding heartbeat wouldn't let him wind down. Everything kept spinning. *Maybe if I know it's a hallucination, I can just accept it's not real and ignore it. But why?* He thought about all the times Shoshana had suggested that he should see a therapist—something she told him not in anger, but out of love—and berated himself for never listening.

He reached into a box of warm beer cans beside the couch, cracked one open, and gulped it down. *Wait, maybe I do know why I'm seeing things. Yeah.* He took another big swig, feeling slightly comforted. *It's because I died. And when I came back, something of... that place, the afterlife, maybe it came back with me. Or maybe it's just my memories. Either way, it's a direct result of dying. Cause and effect. Okay. I can get a handle on this.*

This sounded reasonable to him, but nonetheless, his hands were so shaky that he had to put down his beer. He closed his eyes. In the void of his own mind, he heard people talking. *Just don't listen. Not real. Auditory hallucinations. Ignore them.*

He couldn't.

"I don't want this day to end," the tiny voice of a little boy whimpered. "It's been the best day ever."

"It will end. Everything does," the boy's mother—Axel's mama—replied.

Axel knew these voices and the words they were saying all too well. The memory of the lake house was the one he'd kept closer to his heart than any other. And as he heard it replay in his mind, as his mother once again made him promise to hold onto the memory for the rest of his life, he smelled the sand, water, and pine trees that he'd smelled that night. He heard the water washing up on the shore as the tide drew in, and listened to the crackle of flames in the chiminea. *I'm there again. Even though they're dead, too. Maybe if I... maybe...*

He opened his eyes, hoping to see the lake house, but instead finding himself lost within the dark, dingy living room of a jobless, orphaned widower with a dead son. The memory was just a memory. He exhaled, realizing he'd been holding his breath so long that his lungs hurt. The dead people he loved were so close but just out of reach—and whenever he did try to clasp their memory, they only drew farther away.

Beer in hand, he paced across the apartment. *So, I'm just reliving memories. Nothing cosmic. Maybe that's something to be relieved about. Yeah.* The more he thought about it, the more he preferred the thought of his hallucinations being a result of fatigue and stress, rather than metaphysical in nature. *It's all about anxiety. That's easier to understand, at least. But if I can hear and talk to dead people from my past, then maybe... hmm.* He walked up to the door of what had once—until The Bad Day—been Aaron's room. His chest tightened.

He pushed it open, and as the hinges squeaked, he called out into the forbidden space. "Aaron, kid. You in there?"

He waited. Aaron didn't respond. After hallucinating his dead wife mere moments ago, Axel wasn't sure whether to feel relieved or disappointed.

Axel stepped inside. The room was cold and dusty, lit only by the glowing blue stars and moons stuck to the ceiling, which a little boy had once marveled at every night. The little twin-size bed was perfectly made, with military corners and two pillows. A Superman poster was tacked to the wall, with the same little rip in the bottom right corner that it had had a year ago. Even the mirror on the wall had tiny little fingerprints on it, once touched by tiny little fingers.

Axel slumped into the beanbag across from the bed. "Hey, Aaron. Hope you can hear me," he said. He waited for a voice—*please, please*—and when none came, he took a drink and continued speaking to nobody. "Remember the first day you went to school?"

Again, he waited. He just wanted to hear Aaron's voice one more time—to know he wasn't in the terrible void that Axel had died in earlier that day. *You deserve better than that. A good afterlife, not... that.*

Once again, though, Aaron didn't respond, so Axel continued speaking. "You were scared. Real scared." He drank more beer. "I gave you a big, big hug. We walked you right to the front doors. Walked you in. Shosh, well... she kissed your forehead. Made you feel so loved, that way she always did. You looked at me, though, that little way you always did, so nervous. Said you were worried people wouldn't like you because you were different, and I said... said... shit." Axel took another drink. He couldn't get the words out. He tried to remember the scared, sad look on his little boy's eyes that day and refocused. "I said to you, kid... I said..."

The door creaked open. Axel jumped, and Shoshana, still in her green thrift store bathrobe, stood in the opening. "You said that you had his back," she said. "You said that you were proud of him, and that anytime he was scared, for the rest of his life, he could call you, and you'd drop everything and be there, no matter what."

Axel stared at her, terrified that if he said anything—if he asked a single question about how she had returned—she would vanish again. *This hallucination looks so real. It's gotta be real. Right?*

Shoshana continued. "I loved you so much when you said that," Shoshana said. "Our scared little kid calmed right down, put on such a brave face to make his dad proud. You *always* had such an amazing way of lifting him up... of calming him down, too. Even when he was a baby."

"Yeah," Axel whispered. "That's right."

Shoshana glided across the carpet, sat on the bed across from Axel, and stared at him in the same hyper-focused way that had, over the years, become a source of comfort. As she sat so close to him, he watched her shadow on the floor. He couldn't muster the strength to imagine that she wasn't real. Most of all, he hated the thought of being isolated in Aaron's bedroom, thinking about the dead child that he had so miserably failed and whose body had been lost forever.

"Sorry to be so blunt, Axel," she said, "but you're not okay. Really, *really* not okay."

Axel could lie to Kindred. He could lie to Malik. However, he couldn't lie to her. "You're right," he said. "I'm not okay."

"Heh," Shoshana said. "Loquacious as ever. Take care, Axel. The Stranger is waiting for you."

Axel looked up. Shoshana was gone, and he was alone.

Chapter 7: The Second Death of Axel Rivers

Axel and Shoshana's second apartment, after they got married, was the attic space of an old office building, which had been converted to living spaces. There was limited parking, three flights of stairs, and constant noise from their neighbors, but whenever Axel got home from work, his favorite part of the day was coming back to the little nest they'd created. Even if the day had brought him down, coming home lifted his feelings right back up... on most days.

There was one hot afternoon in July, though, that was different. It hadn't seemed different until he'd opened the front door, started for the stairs, and heard Shoshana's pained sobbing reverberate all the way down.

Axel panicked. He rushed upstairs, flung open the door of their apartment, and raced in to see his wife curled up in the bed, clutching her knees. He reached out to her, and she jerked away from him. "Shoshana —"

"I screwed up." She could barely breathe, crying harder than he'd ever seen her cry before. "Sorry." She sat upright, holding her belly, choking back her anguish.

Axel's stomach dropped through the floor. "Ah, crap." He swallowed. "The baby, is it...?"

"Dead. Goddamn dead." Shoshana groaned, pushing her head back into the pillow. "The ultrasound today showed... underdeveloped... whatever. Fucking useless." She wiped her eyes. "We're having a miscarriage. God, I'm sorry, I'm a mess, I'm sorry that you're with such a mess, I'm sorry —"

Axel gently took her into his arms. She didn't push away this time. He embraced her, and holding back the pain in his heart, he said, "We'll get through this. It'll be okay."

"I'm sorry —"

"Not your fault." He kissed her, trying to focus on what she needed—and not dipping into the well of his own pain. "We read about this, Shosh. Miscarriages happen all the time. They're so common. This has got nothing to do with you, nothing you did wrong, it just happens. Just means that this baby wasn't meant to... to..." He wiped his eyes. "We can try again. If you want. It's up to you. But I'm here for you, no matter what."

"I'm sorry." She sniffled. "I just want a baby so badly, and this... this..."

"Don't be sorry. We're here for each other. Just let me know anything you need—anything you need, baby. I'm here for you, forever."

"I love you," she said. And they held each other, just like that, knowing that no matter what obstacles they faced in the days ahead, they'd always have one other. And as hours turned into days, and days became weeks, as weeks became months, and then a year, a spark of light appeared on a future ultrasound—a baby who would soon squall into the air, give purpose to their tears, and heal all the wounds of the past.

When that baby was born, they named him Aaron.

AXEL RIVERS HAD RARELY—IF ever—slept well since being in the military, but that night, he barely slept at all. Between dying for the first time and then hallucinating his dead wife, his scattered moments of rest were punctuated by nightmares of the hooded Stranger, with its mangled hand, clutching his throat.

At 3:15 a.m., he gave up on the idea of rest. He exited his room, and while his original intention had been to sit on the porch and stare out at the parking lot, he wasn't sure if he'd put the gun away or if it was still out there. If the latter was true, he didn't want to find out.

So, instead, he cleaned the apartment. Every surface was scrubbed. The carpet was vacuumed. Aaron's room was dusted. At one point, he even considered packing away the contents of Shoshana's dresser and closet, none of which—from her makeup to her jewelry and clothes—had been touched since her death, down to the mountainous pile of random items covering the dresser's surface. This endeavor collapsed when, as he sorted through that pile, a folded note emerged—with the words "Dear Axel…" written on the top.

His heart caught in his throat. He tucked the note back under the pile. He was terrified of getting his hopes up, unfolding it, and finding that it was just an unfinished note that she'd abandoned before leaving the apartment on that last day. *Or something she wrote when she was angry. Odds are pretty good on that one.*

By the time he'd made it onto the bus for his second trip to Kindred Eternal Solutions, staying awake had become more of a challenge. Every time he dozed off, though, he was awoken by visions of the Stranger. During one of these wakeups, he'd tried to distract himself by looking into the cars driving beside the bus. One driver was doing her makeup as she tailgated another. The driver behind her was an elderly man, trying to drink coffee as he switched lanes with no signal. All around them, Axel spotted people looking at their cell phones as they drove. Weaving. Not paying attention. One of the texting drivers had two kids in the back seat, and at the sight of this, Axel's stomach lurched. He wanted to slam the window and tell the driver to put their phone down, but realized anything he did would only increase the odds of an accident, rather than prevent one. *All of them are going to die anyway,* he thought. *All of them are going to the same place I did yesterday. Where they'll find nothing good.*

His phone buzzed, and to his dismay, it flashed another old photo of Aaron. This time, the little boy was jumping into a giant puddle of rain.

Axel shuddered as he thought about The Bad Day. *Did you call out for me on that day, Aaron?* The thought chilled him. He imagined Aaron screaming "Daddy! Daddy!" as water swept him away, filled his lungs, and stole his life. *But who knows. He could've been crying for Mommy instead. At least Mommy was there with him. I wasn't. Hell, if I were him, I probably would've called for Mommy.*

The bus stopped. Passengers unloaded. It was time to die again.

AS A NEWBORN, LITTLE Aaron had clung to his mother, like any newborn does. The mother is the home. The place and person of utmost safety. Somewhere around nine months, though, there came a point where, at nighttime, Axel was the one who Aaron felt most comfortable falling asleep with, and these moments shared between father and son became the highlight of Axel's days.

Every night, a few hours after getting home from work, Axel rocked Aaron to sleep in his arms. "Shhh," he'd whisper as the tiny eyes of the tiny creature in his arms gazed unblinkingly at his. Sometimes, Aaron smiled. Other times, with increasing regularity, he'd coo, twist his neck back, and string together weird sounds. Occasionally, he pulled hard on Axel's beard, with surprising strength, and giggled when his daddy's face came close.

"You got me, Aaron," Axel would say, laughing with him. "Daddy loves you."

Aaron's sweetness, his desperate need to always be held, was both heartwarming and heartbreaking. Axel got to know when Aaron was tired, even when he didn't seem like he was. He felt it with an almost psychic assuredness. Holding Aaron's tiny, chubby, oh-so-vulnerable little body, he often felt overwhelmed by the fact that here, in his lap, was a life that he'd co-created. It seemed amazing to think that over the centuries of human existence, babies had been born and would continue to be born in the future. Holding Aaron felt like the end of Axel's story—that his cycle was in its final chapter, and he was passing the baton onward. It was a good feeling. It meant that, despite everything in the past, he'd succeeded.

Whenever Aaron cried, Axel sang to him, and fairly often, he hummed the tune of his mother's mysterious song—"Ending Forever." He didn't know the words. He'd never learned Khmer, and since there were no written lyrics, it was a moot point. However, he did know that if he kept the tune alive and passed it on to this beautiful child, then a piece of his family history would live on past the car wreck that had claimed his own parents.

"Love you," he repeated, kissing Aaron's soft, sleeping cheek.

AXEL WAITED IN THE medical room where he'd soon be killed, shivering with anticipation. He'd been waiting for nearly ten minutes, and in his desperation not to think about death, he'd examined every tiny detail around him, from the strange machinery to the paperwork left on the counter. He didn't look too closely—a security camera was clearly attached to the ceiling, and it occasionally blinked like a warning shot—but he did notice that the paper-clipped stack had a sticky note on the front, addressed to Dr. Kendra Carpenter, with a casualness that seemed bewildering to him in this setting:

Kendra, here are the files you requested, re: Deathscape reports. Let me know if I missed anything. A propos, a bunch of the docs are going out for drinks again later. You want to join us? We can pick you up, if you like. Your address is 888A Fifth Street, right? Let me know, so I can put it in my phone.

—M.

Axel shook his head at the normalcy of it all. *Intentional disconnect from their setting,* he thought. *They try to act as if nothing's unusual, to connect to other humans in the most normal way possible, as a way to disassociate from the weird shit they do at work. Wasn't any different in the military, remember?* Before he could think much more on it, Dr. Carpenter herself entered. He didn't mention the note, since he didn't want to get anybody in trouble, but he did wave hello. "Morning," he said.

"Good morning, Axel." She checked her clipboard. "Did you sleep okay?" She pulled the board down, and while her mouth was masked, her eyes were smiling. "Just kidding, of course."

Axel smirked. "Guess you know the answer. Nobody sleeps the first night, huh?"

"Not a soul."

After this nice moment, the other doctors entered, and the traumas from the day before were reopened. Axel was strapped down, plugged in, and made to look at the red light. He tried to swallow his panic—to tell himself that this was no different than being drugged—but his body knew differently. *I should shout that I don't want this. Walk away. Forget about the cash.* The thought that it might be too late to walk only scared him further.

"Dr. Carpenter," he said, desperately linking eyes with her, and studying her expression for clues. "Last time, I saw something. It was called the Stranger. I think it talked to me? Or something. And last night, when I got home, I saw people who were—"

"Dead?" She glanced at her coworker. "Yes, Axel, that's a normal side effect. It can be difficult for the human mind to move between death and life after experiencing the Deathscape for the first time, since we all carry over so much psychological baggage—"

"What is the Stranger?" He frowned. "Wait. And what's that word you said? Deathscape?"

Dr. Carpenter didn't answer either query. She plunged the needle in, and Axel jerked against his restraints then slumped downward as his heart fluttered to a stop. Once again, the sound of rushing water filled his ears. Colors faded. Everything went dark, and he died for the second time in his life.

NOTHINGNESS.

The needle injects nothingness into Axel's veins, and soon, there are no veins and no needle. As Axel dies again, his consciousness is decimated. Fragments of soul break into smaller and smaller pieces, becoming dust in the void. Once again, the emptiness is overwhelming. His senses have disappeared. His identity no longer exists. There is no Axel Rivers. Nothing is there. Nothing, except...

Water. He feels it coursing through whatever has become. He hears it crashing against unseen rocks. It sounds real. More real, perhaps, than anything has ever sounded since he was a child first discovering the world.

He realizes, then, that he is a child again. He is a new being. *I'm starting over.* He opens a set of eyes that he has never opened before, and he sees ultraviolet colors crashing against the nothingness. His new limbs—the same ones he felt last time—pop outward. He feels that he can choose the shape of these appendages—he could develop claws or tentacles if he wanted—but the thought of this is too alarming for him, and so they snap into human limbs instead.

The water crashes into his body. It crushes his sides. Fills his ears. He is drowning. *Like Aaron and Shoshana drowned on The Bad Day.* Then he opens his lungs—his *new* lungs—and realizes the water is warm. Sweet. Thick. More like honey than water. He paddles through whatever substance he is mixed into, and his fingertips press against something spongy, textured, and wet.

I know this. He sees it with his new eyes. He is inside an amniotic sac.

He digs his nails into the surface. They break through the sac's skin. Fractalized shards of energy flood into the darkness, and as he bursts free into the bottom of an iridescent turquoise ocean, he sees millions—billions—of other sacs, just like it, like giant fish eggs. He kicks away the remains of his carrier vessel. He pushes upward. Up, up, up, until he crashes through the surface of the water and gasps for air—air that is cleaner, crisper, filled with life and movement unlike any air he has ever breathed.

Axel is dead, but he feels alive. More alive than he's ever felt.

The cascading colors, lights, energies, and shapes surrounding him above the water are too much to comprehend. His eyes—still raw, spongy, freshly grown—can't process the information. He swims to the edge of the water and climbs onto the shore. Beneath the rocks is not sand nor dirt but a spongy, textured, wriggling surface, humming with electricity. *Gray matter,* he realizes, as he feels it carefully. *I'm on top of a giant brain. My brain? Hell if I know. This is some ludicrous stuff.*

Slowly, his eyes craft a visible recreation of the world that exists around him. The first thing he recognizes is the rocks on the shore. *Those look normal. Okay, that's cool. Helps me piece it together.* He then absorbs the sight of the glowing turquoise water—rustling in a perfect, calming manner—and notes how fractalized particles emit from its surface like steam. The temperature of the air, he feels, is impossibly perfect. Slowly, the sky becomes visible to him.

"Wow," he whispers. "So, this is the Deathscape."

The atmosphere surrounding him is the entirety of the universe. Billions of galaxies spin around his tiny body. Suns explode. Asteroids crash into planets. All of it is so distant but so close, and so simultaneous, that he can only perceive little parts of it, yet never focus fully on one thing at a time. Clouds of ultraviolet energies, unlike any colors he has ever seen when alive, rush all around him.

And standing at the very center of this dimension, towering above everything else that exists, is a colossal tree.

The great tree is so incomprehensibly huge that Axel can't think of anything remotely similar. It dwarfs the Northern California redwoods. It makes the Empire State Building look like a pin. The tree is bigger than a mountain—perhaps even bigger than the Earth itself. Its branches spread across the cosmos. Its roots stretch across the entire landscape, twisting and breathing like wooden snakes. The tree's bark is black, but it shimmers gold, and it's easily the most impossibly beautiful thing Axel has ever seen.

"Amazing." Axel stares upward, unable to do anything but marvel, awestruck, at what is before him. He approaches the nearest root, mesmerized by the realization that even this one tiny section of it, jutting out from the gray-matter earth, is bigger than his entire apartment building.

The root breathes in and out like an elephant. He touches the wood. It hums beneath his hand. The bark's texture is composed of an infinite number of complex geometric shapes, twisted together, which tightly cling to his hand. He pulls away in surprise, and a shimmering handprint remains in its place, with the swirl of a fossilized nautilus shell in its center.

"Damn," he mutters, examining his mark. "Wish I knew what any of this meant."

The handprint becomes permanently etched into the wood. From it, a glowing white flower sprouts in fast motion. The flower's petals flutter, and shimmering tendrils snake down from it, embracing the root. Sparkling fractals spiral outward from the flower's center. Axel pauses to stare at this. *It's the flower from Kindred's orientation video. That's crazy. And it means...* He clenches his fists. *It means they know this place. Kindred has been here.*

Axel wanders away in a daze. *So much to take in.* He follows the shoreline, and he notes a blue glow that emanates from a square block dug into the ground. *That doesn't look right.* As he approaches this light, he realizes what's wrong about it—it's man-made. It is a metal square, with rivets and screws, embedded in the gray matter, with the glowing blue KINDRED ETERNAL SOLUTIONS logo composed of many tiny blue lightbulbs.

"Huh."

The back of his neck itches. Coldness passes over him. He stares at the KINDRED logo for a second longer—*it's like corporate graffiti*—and as he turns around, everything blinks away then blinks back. *Shit.* His ears ring with the high-pitched whining noise he heard in his first death. *Oh no.* He buckles forward, clenching his ears, as the cacophony splits through his head. By the time the noise softens, he's so overwhelmed that he barely notices the Stranger looming over him.

Axel jolts back, nearly falling into the water. The robed apparition stands there, unmoving, not speaking, its face shaded by its tattered hood. Axel's entire body tenses up in the Stranger's presence. *Run away.* He looks around, but he sees that he has nowhere to run to. *You're dead. You're here in the Stranger's house. There is no getting away.* He inhales the now-icy air, and he feels his body—his new body—become cold, mushy, and corpselike.

"What do you want?" Axel says in a trembling voice.

The Stranger points at him with its destroyed hand, blood dripping from severed fingertips. It says nothing. The sky goes from transparent to opaque. Cold rain droplets speckle downward. The Stranger lowers its dark hood, revealing a plastic mask has been nailed to its face—a mask that, despite its cheap appearance, is clearly modeled after the crying face of Aaron Rivers.

Axel nearly screams in horror, but he can't look away. *Aaron.* Giant cartoon tears drip down the mask's molded cheeks. A burnt gash runs through the mask's center, splitting Aaron's face in two. Behind the two eyeholes, there is nothing but empty darkness.

"You're not Aaron." Axel steps back and trips over a small root.

The Stranger's robe opens at the front, revealing a body of mud, roots, and flowers. Curled up in the Stranger's chest, buried within it,

Axel sees the decomposed skeleton of a child, and he is so horrified that his mind goes blank. He feels the Stranger's nonexistent eyes bore into him, and he remembers the last time he saw Aaron. *He asked me to come with him. I said no.*

A scratchy voice emits from behind the Stranger's plastic mask. "Your fault."

Chapter 8: The Deathweavers

"Tell me if you're Aaron." Axel asks, hating every word that escapes his lips. "Don't let me wonder."

Standing in the landscape of death—surrounded by spinning galaxies, ultraviolet clouds, and a tree with infinitely long branches stretching between the folds of the universe—Axel can no longer see anything but the bizarre figure before him, with its black robe and a cracked, plastic mask depicting the visage of his sobbing son. *That can't be Aaron. This can't be his eternal fate. Please, no.* Axel feels himself wavering, and so he locks his emotions away until he is like stone. He refuses to let the entity before him crack open his deepest pain. *It's not Aaron. Can't be. Won't accept it.*

The Stranger answers in a voice so empty it makes Axel shudder. "Too late."

The Stranger reaches toward Axel with its bleeding hand. He ducks away but loses his footing and crashes backward into one of the roots from the cosmic tree. "Aaron, if that's you..." he starts but can't bring himself to finish. The ground rumbles beneath him.

The high-pitched whine pierces his ears again. He closes his eyes in pain, but instead of meeting darkness behind his eyelids, he sees white—and then, behind the white, he finds himself in a new place altogether.

"What... where?" He shakes his head. "Huh?"

The natural landscape of roots, branches, water, and outer space has been replaced by a cityscape of crystalline towers. A metropolis of glass.

He stands in the central block as giant billboards flash blue KINDRED logos at his eyes. The streets are empty, and as he steps forward, gems crackle beneath his heels. He sees electrical cords wrapped around the bases of the glass towers. No people, no life, no plants, but signs of civilization—an empty civilization, either abandoned or not yet populated—everywhere he turns. Far in the distance, far in the mountains, is the Deathscape, where the Great Tree wraps its branches into the sky, but what once was so close is now beyond reach.

"Where the hell...?" He looks up. The Stranger is floating over him, glaring down from the eyeless holes in its mask.

"Here," the Stranger says, "is where you end."

The horrible whine amplifies. Axel holds his ears, screaming, as the Stranger drops before him. The whine echoes between the reflective structures surrounding him—*it comes from the glass, somehow*—and he crumples down into the shimmering pavement. It cracks open, pulling him underneath, devouring his body. He is sucked deep into the earth. Darkness starts to overcome him.

Somewhere, on another level of reality, he feels his heart—his earthly heart—beating rapidly. The doctors are reviving him.

"Are you really Aaron?" he grunts through the pain.

The Stranger says nothing. Axel's heart speeds up faster. He clenches his fists. *No. I won't let them take me back. Not without Aaron. If this is Aaron. If.*

"I won't go without Aaron!" he screams into the Glass City, blocking out the fluorescent lights of the living world attempting to flood into his eyes. The darkness closes in again. He kicks madly. He fights against his resurrection.

"Wake up, Axel," a voice says. "Ah, damn it..."

AXEL'S EYES OPENED, and he saw Dr. Carpenter standing over him. "Wake up, Axel." She shook him. "Ah, damn it..." She looked at the computer screen. "He's fighting the resurrection."

Axel held his breath until his lungs felt like water balloons on the brink of popping. He clenched his eyes, focused, and resisted. *Don't let go. Don't come back to life. Not without Aaron. Not without talking to him. Apologizing.*

"Axel, listen to my voice and..."

Axel faded out.

AXEL IS DEAD AGAIN.

He is no longer in the Glass City.

Now, his body is comfortably nestled in a tangle of the Great Tree's roots—moving vines cradling him like an infant. He stands up, rubbing his sore head, and peers out over the horizon of the Deathscape. While the Glass City still shimmers from a faraway valley, he has returned to the natural wonders of the Deathscape.

Axel gazes out at the Glass City in the distance. *Aaron. He's still out there.* "Hey!" he shouts at the top of his lungs. "Come back and talk to me!"

A soft hand falls on Axel's shoulder. "The Stranger can't hear you," Shoshana says.

Axel flips around to see the freckled face of his wife. "Hey," he whispers in astonishment. His wife's skin, eyes, and hair possess a silvery glow, and light emits from her every exhalation—it is Shoshana, unquestionably, but not quite the same Shoshana whom he had once spent his early mornings wrapped in the arms of. Axel gapes in awe at her. *I can't believe it. Say something, Axel. Speak. Tell her how much she means to you.* "Shoshana... you're here" is all he can push out from his lips, and immediately feels that his words are profoundly lacking. He reaches out to embrace her.

"Wait." She holds out a hand. "I'm not what you think I am."

He stops, his heart fizzling with a soggy mixture of disappointment, understanding, and confusion. He steps backward, colliding with a giant root. Steadying himself, he briefly considers sitting on the root, but decides against it, feeling that it would be offensive to sit on something so sacred.

"The real Shoshana, the one you loved and married..." the woman says, taking his face into her cool hands. "She has passed on to the next stage and become one with all of the universe. Pieces of her remain, both in everything she ever touched, and in worlds and galaxies she never imagined. Some of those pieces stayed with you. Those pieces are me. And these are the pieces that all creatures leave with all the other creatures who ever loved them, as you so deeply loved her. But the totality of Shoshana, I—"

"So, you're not her." Axel says. "That fucking sucks." He rubs his head, feeling like an idiot. "Sorry. Don't mean to be rude."

"I am her, but I'm not her in the way you thought, no," she says, "But only *part* of her, because the entirety of her is far greater than me alone."

Axel again fights the temptation to sit down. What she is saying makes sense, but it feels unreal to hear such things in such an unearthly setting, instead of a meditation circle or a spirituality book. As Shoshana stares inquisitively at him, Axel shrinks even deeper into himself. "Sorry, just that I want to tell her—the real her. Want her to know how much I regret screwing up everything we—"

She covers his mouth, in a playful manner that completely lines with the Shoshana he knows. "The universe does not care about your self-admonishment, Axel."

He grins. "Now that sounds like something Shoshana would say."

"Fair enough." She seems less amused. "Axel, we don't have much time. Kindred is about to revive you, within the next 30 minutes. You were able to push them off the one time, before I rescued you from the Stranger—"

"You're the reason I appeared here?"

"Yes, but your heart is going to be jump-started any minute now, and while we have this brief moment, I need you to stop looking at this world—stop, and listen. Listen carefully." She waits and then narrows her eyes. "No, *listen*."

His ears ring gently. *I don't understand.* He stares into her eyes, and as she smiles, his sense of hearing expands outward, as if two shells over his ears have just fallen away to reveal deeper, more powerful tunnels beneath. *Okay. Okay, I hear a scratching sound.* He listens more concentratedly. *No, it's... a drawing sound. Pen on paper.* "What is that?" he asks.

"Shh," Shoshana whispers. "It's the Deathweavers."

Axel pulls back from her. The sheer phrase—*Deathweavers*—startles him with its power. *Feels like déjà vu. Like I've heard it before, or sensed it. But I haven't.* He closes his eyes, trying to understand the chills running down him and wondering if maybe it's because some part of this experience—the Deathscape, the Deathweavers—has always been inside him. *Inside everyone. Or outside? Hell if I know.*

"Deathweavers?" he asks hesitantly. "Wait, why are you telling me this? Everyone's so goddamn mysterious, and then you just reveal something so loaded."

"Because the original Shoshana, who climbed up there long ago—" She points up to the topmost branches of the Great Tree. "Whatever part of her is in me, that still lives in you, is telling me... no, *demanding*, that you need to know about the Deathweavers. The universe follows a path, and evidently, it has been decided that it involves an unprecedented collision between you and them." She casts her eyes downward. "Before you ask me, I don't understand why. I have told you what I know."

Axel gazes up at the branches longingly, as he imagines Shoshana scaling up to them and disappearing into the light. He felt happy, looking up there. Serene. *The top of the tree. That's where we all really go. The true afterlife.* "So this place down here, this whole Deathscape, it's just an in-between place. Not the end. Something like that."

"Something like that," Shoshana agrees, taking his hand and walking him away from the roots. "You are not fully dead, Axel Rivers. No one here is. When your final death and assimilation into The Everything truly happens, there can be no resurrection back to your original corporeal form—Kindred or not."

As they walk, Axel eyes a root that has been marred by a glowing blue KINDRED logo, carved into the wood. *Creepy corporate assholes...* He stops, glances out at the Glass City on the horizon, then continues following Shoshana's lead as she guides him down a winding path of hazy ultraviolet clouds. "So, what's it like at the top of the tree? Is that where I could talk to—"

"There is honestly no way for me to describe it to you that could ever be satisfying, until you find your own way there." Shoshana continues pulling him along as they climb onto a root and follow it over a roaring turquoise river. "It's not going to be anything like the way you envision it. When you climb into the topmost branches, Axel, every thought, experience, and action of your life merges with the actions and feelings of every other being who has ever lived and died. Your contributions are sewn together with the fabric of reality, creating a greater whole. Everything that was once *you*—you, as a singular entity—spreads out to become a part of everything that still remains, but it's not that your consciousness breaks up—it just expands, and expands and expands, to take in all the numerous experiences that your collective mind is now joined to. You take your place as part of The Everything."

"Well, damn." He shakes his head. "I *think* that sounds relieving?"

"You'll find out." She smiles then shakes her head and leads them up a rocky hill. "It's physical, too. Remember the Law of Conservation of Energy that I talked about on the night we first met?"

"Energy can't be created or destroyed."

"Right. Use that as an anchor to understand what I'm saying. So, then, once the original Shoshana joined The Everything, the parts of Shoshana that were connected to the people and things she loved expanded outward, and have continued to live on in the physical realm. When you think of her, and remember her, when you look at a photo, you are breathing her essence in. You are genuinely sharing a moment with her. Not in some made-up, fanciful way—it's *truly* her. Truly me." She gazes at him for a moment, lips pursed, and Axel fights the urge to kiss her. "But only part of her. Albeit a pretty important part. The same is true for everyone she ever touched in her life. Even that homeless man on the subway she once gave a $50 bill to. He still remembers her. A tiny part of her—of me—lives on in him, as well, because of that."

"Huh. Thanks for actually explaining things to me. Even if it's hard to understand." He smiles. *She was nice to a lot of people, so that's a lot of pieces.* "Got another question, though. What about you? This part of her that you are. Do you climb the tree too, since you're... whatever you are?"

They are nearing the crest of the hill. "Yes, because I am alive, you know. When your journey ends, your memories of her—me—will climb as well, and also join with The Everything. And now, Axel—" She stops as they reach the peak. "Look." She points downward. "These are the Deathweavers."

Axel steps to the edge, looks down upon a gorgeous beach of black sand, and then pulls back in fear. "Damn." He rubs his eyes. *So much to take in. Everything here is.* He looks again. Spread across the length of the beach are hundreds of octopus-like creatures, each one the size of a human. Their skin perfectly reflects the lights of the universe, as if every one of them contains their own galaxy, and in place of their heart is a glowing white sun.

Surrounding each of these Deathweavers is a circular arrangement of creative tools. Far in the distance, he sees Deathweavers operating enormous looms. *Fits their name, I guess. Wonder if they were the first ones.* On other stretches of the beach, there are Deathweavers playing multiple musical instruments at once—a guitar, a piano, a cello, a flute, each artistic tool operated by a different starry appendage. Some Deathweavers make shapes out of smoke, while others plant perfectly symmetrical gardens, and still more place seashells in strange geometric configurations.

The row of Deathweavers which stand closest to Axel, though, appear to have chosen drawing as their passion. *Okay, ink on paper. They're the ones I heard before.* Each one of these Deathweavers is surrounded by a perfect circle of giant sketchbooks, laid flat on the black sand—a sketchbook for every individual tentacle. As Axel steps closer, he is astonished to realize that these Deathweavers are drawing on all their sketchbooks simultaneously, with each tentacle gripping its own little pen.

"They're..." Axel swallows. "Kinda beautiful. In a weird-as-hell way."

Shoshana smiles and nods. "They certainly are." She gestures for Axel to walk ahead of her, and so he climbs down the hill until he is standing on the same black beach. The sketchbook Deathweavers take no notice of him. Their circular heads, filled with dozens of glistening dark eyes, are constantly spinning to examine all of their sketches, while multiple pens jab at multiple papers in whip-like motions. They are frenetically busy, but not tired. He can only assume that they don't sleep.

Axel stares along the length of the beach, mesmerized by how each Deathweaver works so intently on so many projects. Then he hesitantly approaches the nearest creature and waves at it. "Hey," he says, feeling stupid when the Deathweaver does not respond. "Ah... hello?" The

Deathweaver's eyes do not even flicker in his direction. Shoshana nudges him gently. "What?" he asks.

"Don't take offense. If they have a choice, they will not pay any attention to you. Their work is too important. That's why I'm personally finding it really confusing to understand why I was supposed to bring you to them."

"No kidding." He frowns. "What's the point of being here? And what the hell are they so busy with?"

Shoshana leans close and then whispers into his ear, as if breaking an unspoken rule. "They are the ones who decide when and how every living creature in existence is born or reborn, and they decide when those same creatures must die. They are the only ones on this level who have memorized the eternal pattern. They maintain infinite balance. Without them guiding every level below this one, the universe would fall apart."

"This level. Huh." Axel nudges upward. "Tell me, is there something up there on the next level that knows all this stuff, too? Some sort of... ah, higher power? A God. Or multiple gods. You know. Or something similar."

Shoshana smiles from the side of her mouth. "I don't *know*, Axel. That's way above my head. *I'm* not composed of the parts of Shoshana that exist up there now, so I can't answer that in any tangible way. Maybe? It feels likely. Probably depends on your perception." She points back at the Deathweavers. "For now, just pay attention to them, and let's try to figure out why I had to bring you here."

Axel shrugs, then he steps even closer to the nearest Deathweaver. It continues to ignore his presence. He leans over one of its pads of paper—a slick black tentacle whipping a pen across the page just inches from his nose—and sees that the drawings depict a mind-bogglingly complex array of geometric shapes, symbols, arrows, and equations, all of them perfectly connected in a myriad of ways. "Huh." He then steps over to another page and notices how on this drawing, the Deathweaver is somehow erasing the ink from the corner of the page and then drawing new shapes in the empty spot's place.

He turns around. "They can change things."

"They *constantly* change things," Shoshana replies. "Nothing they do is random. In determining the death of every creature in existence, throughout all of history, there are rules they must follow to assert cosmic balance—maintaining this requires following complex equations, which only they understand. Maybe, for instance, when one person is to be born, three must die on the same day. Only they know why. Maybe one person must develop a terrible disease, such as Alzheimer's, in order for another person to not starve to death on the wrong day, which may itself unravel another important part of the universe. All of it is multifaceted, intricate... everything has to fit together just right."

"They can give someone Alzheimer's on a certain day so that someone else doesn't, or does, die on a different day. Seriously? They have that kinda power?"

"Yes. Everything—*everything*—is linked, Axel. And only they can make the trades and switches necessary to keep those links intact. Death and birth are at the center of it all."

Axel ponders something. *Hmm. Maybe if...* "What about changing the past? Maybe they could bring back someone who has already died."

Shoshana's eyes sadden. She takes Axel's hand. He shivers. *This is only part of Shoshana. Not the full person. Remember that.* "No," she says softly. "They can't change what already happened. They can only change what will occur. There's no bringing back your wife and son."

Axel's heart sinks. He walks around the Deathweaver, watching it carefully. *This is so goddamn crazy.* He closes his eyes. "Man. This is a lot to take in. And the Stranger... what the hell is that?"

Shoshana's eyes widen.

"Shoshana," he repeats. "What is the Stranger? Is it Aaron?"

She says something, but her words are indecipherable gibberish. It's as if her voice has been replaced with white noise. Her face is overtaken by fear.

"Shoshana?" he asks frenetically. Sparks shoot from her skin. "Shoshana!"

A tear appears in her eye. "It is... isn't... is..." She shakes her head, and she speaks in white noise again. After several false starts, she is able to slowly mouth the words, "You're waking up, Axel. I'm losing my connection to you."

Shit. He sees the Deathscape blinking away. "Tell me what the Stranger is before you go," he says.

"Can't... Stranger..." Her voice fades out. "I see now. I see why you had to meet the Deathweavers! You have to come back here, but... don't... don't trust..." She trails off, and then her voice returns. "Can't save..." Everything sounds mumbled. Then he hears her saying something that makes no sense to him. "Maybe... maybe, you could save *her*, though." Her eyes open wider. "Trade *her*. But you'll have to sacrifice something beautiful, if they even allow it... sounds impossible..."

"Shoshana!" he calls out, feeling sick to his stomach. "I can't understand what you're saying!"

The world darkens around him. The Deathweavers disappear. The beach vanishes. Shoshana blinks out of existence, and colors and shapes become more solid, less wondrous. And through the darkness, he hears the voice of Dr. Kendra Carpenter calling for him to come back. "Jesus Christ, Axel, we almost lost you. Wake up."

This time, he can't stop himself from blinking back to life.

AN HOUR HAD PASSED.

Axel stood outside of the Kindred building, waiting for the bus. Despite the relatively warm temperature—particularly compared to the past week—he felt terribly cold and nauseous. *Side effect of dying two times in one day, Dr. Carpenter said.* Visions of what he'd seen that day, from the menace of the Stranger, to the splendor of the Great Tree and Shoshana, to the eerie comfort of the Deathweavers, were running through his mind's eye, making it hard to concentrate on the solid world he now faced.

It sure as hell didn't feel like a dream. He pressed his feet to the ground. *It felt realer than any of this does. Like all of this is a lie, and that's the real world. Feels like violating something to allow Kindred to yank me in and out of that place, though. Maybe I should quit this messed up program.*

He paused, catching himself. The truth was, he *wanted* to go back—to die again. *What does that say about me?* The Deathscape terrified him. The realization that he'd have to face the Stranger again terrified him even more, and the more he thought about it, the clearer the Stranger's identity seemed to become. *I have to go back. If there's anything of Aaron in the Stranger, I have to reach out to him. To save him. Because maybe... maybe the Stranger is also comprised of my memories of Aaron—maybe because I've been so goddamn afraid of facing that kid's death, I've turned these pieces of him into a monster. Maybe. Or maybe I'm just a dumbass Earthling trying to make sense of some cosmic shit that's way above my pay grade.* Either way, the possibilities only deepened the cold terror within him.

A familiar voice spoke to him, and it took him a moment to recognize it as Brooklyn—much less piece together the words she was saying. "Hi, Battle-ax. You okay?" she said. Brooklyn's eyes, with her uneven pupils, were reddened with tears. "Bet you're as freaked out as I am."

Once Axel remembered where he was, he couldn't figure out what to say. He simply shrugged. After a long and tense moment, he forced out the first thought that occurred to him, and immediately regretted it. "Hey, gotta ask. What's the story with your eyes?"

"Everybody has to ask." She stared at him with her alien gaze then pointed at her big, black pupil, followed by the tiny one. "Anisocoria. For me, this was caused by trauma to the eye."

"Trauma."

"Yeah," she laughed uncomfortably. "In other words, my first ex-boyfriend beat my face in, and that's one of the marks that never went away. Not the only mark he left." She sighed. "Wasn't the only ex who beat me, either. Sorry, this is awkward. You don't want to hear this. We just fucking died today, for the second goddamn time. Maybe we should talk about that instead."

Axel tensed up. Despite barely knowing the woman, hearing that somebody had mistreated her like that made him feel extremely protective of her. *Wish I had something to say. Something to help.* As the bus pulled up, Axel nudged her. "We're all going to die someday," he said. "You're right. Should talk about it. Maybe with beer."

She hesitantly smiled. "You want to get that drink this time?"

"Walking distance, right?"

She nodded. "Walking distance."

Chapter 9: Here on Planet Earth

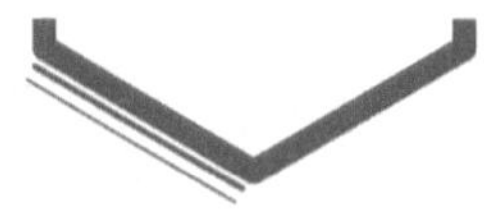

"I'm scared, Daddy."

Aaron hid behind his father's leg, his tiny hands gripping Axel's jeans tightly. The door of the pediatrician's office was only a few steps away. Axel sighed—holding back the tired, but amused chuckle that parents have when a kid is making an easy situation difficult, but doing so in an undeniably cute way—and he crouched down to meet his son's eye level. "C'mon. What's a tough guy like you afraid of?"

"Doctors." Aaron stared downward.

"What's so scary about doctors? You've seen Dr. Cromwell your whole life. He's a really nice guy."

"Um, I saw a movie once, late at night, that you and Mommy were watching... I don't know, it was scary. The doctor had this big needle." Aaron shuddered, clutching his father even tighter. "He had electricity, too. It turned people into zombies, and... and..."

"Great." Axel laughed. "That was just a movie, kid. Nothing to worry about. All fake."

"Do you like going to the doctor, though?"

"I guess not." Axel turned to the doors, eyeing the receptionist. "But it's good for us to go, y'know. The doctors make sure we're going to be healthy, safe, all that stuff. It's just like last week, when I was checking everything out under the hood of my car, remember? If you don't check on things, and take care of them, you can lose them. I mean... wouldn't you hate it if I got sick, and we didn't know, because I didn't want to go to the doctor?"

Aaron hugged him tightly. "I would hate that."

"Same here." Axel snuggled with him for a moment. "So, tell you what. How about every time either of us goes, we go together, to take care of each other, okay? If Dr. Cromwell pulls out some big needle or electricity machine and tries to turn you into a zombie, kid, I've got your back. Deal?"

Aaron smiled. "Deal."

Aaron took Axel's hand, and they went inside together. As they did so, Axel's phone rang, and he sighed—but this time, with no undercurrent of amusement. It was Shoshana, probably calling about the argument they'd had last night. She wanted to talk. Axel didn't... or, well, he did, but he couldn't find the words to explain himself, and it was easier to just let time pass. He knew that was a bad way to deal with problems. He also knew he'd have to open up to her at some point—to admit to her that, despite the life they'd built, the adventures they'd had together, and how much she'd helped him, he was now feeling his old depression kicking in—but he didn't want to talk about it yet.

He didn't answer the phone.

THE BAR KNOWN AS BEELZE Brews was a well-kept secret. It had no signs and no windows—from the outside, it didn't exist. And even on the inside, it had the vibe of a place that somehow existed between planes of reality, locked away by a magical password.

Beelze Brews had no parking, no security, only one bartender, and a handful of patrons spread far apart. Its single-room exterior was long and bizarrely narrow, its cave-like atmosphere augmented by concrete walls, moody lighting, and a grungy vibe that would've seemed trendy if it wasn't forced by rather obvious budgetary constraints. On the far end, an older couple played darts. In the middle, three male friends watched the television behind the bar, where—ironically enough—Kevin Tyler, the trillionaire head of Kindred Eternal Solutions, was giving an interview on late-night TV.

Meanwhile, at the corner of the bar closest to the tinted windows, Axel and Brooklyn sat together, feeling comfortably isolated. To Axel, it was a nice feeling. After months of lonely nights spent drinking countless beer cans at home by himself, it was nice to share a glass with someone else.

"Whatever you say, Battle-ax." Brooklyn laughed, midway through gulping down her cold beer. Froth remained on her upper lip. "I'm telling you, there's no way these assholes at Kindred actually screen people. It's all a sham."

Axel laughed with her—a sensation that felt weird and foreign after the past year. He was already feeling buzzed. "Got a mustache." He pointed at his mouth then hers.

"You mean—? Oh. Oops." She wiped the froth away. "Honestly, though, I'm serious. Like, dead serious." She stopped, then grinned even winder. "Okay, bad choice of words."

Axel chuckled again. "Yep."

"Yeah." She clinked glasses with him. "But trust me, man. Nobody *actually* gets screened out of this Kindred thing, despite all the psych tests, psych sessions, background checks, and other junk. Kindred just pretends to do screenings, probably for legal reasons or whatever, but when it comes down to it? They accept anybody."

Axel sipped his beer. "Nah." He paused to weigh his words. "They do the psych screenings for a purpose. They have to screen out people who are, y'know..."

"What, damaged people?" Brooklyn raised an eyebrow. "In other words, people like *us*? Because we didn't get screened out, and that's my whole point."

Axel tried not to feel offended, but her words chafed him. He took another drink, but before he could defend himself, Brooklyn rolled up the sleeve of her hoodie and removed her wristband. "Come on, Brooklyn," Axel said, turning away. "You don't have to do that."

"No," she answered, and dropped her bare wrist onto the table before him. "I'm not afraid to be truthful. Don't be afraid to look."

Her wrist was a patchwork quilt of scars. The razor blade had left so many signatures in her flesh that he couldn't even count them all. *Holy shit.* Most were thin lines, but others were so puffy—and jagged—that even gazing at them made him wince.

Axel squeezed her wrist in both his hands. "I'm sorry," he said. "Whatever you went through that made you feel like you had to do this..." He paused, examining the scars again. "These are all old. Nothing fresh."

"You bet." With a vulnerable look in her eye, Brooklyn squeezed his hand briefly, and she then rolled her sleeve back up. "That's because I stopped cutting as soon as I became pregnant with my daughter."

Axel flinched. "You have a daughter?"

"Yeah. Gwendolyn. Shit, I didn't mention her yet? She's six years old. Most amazing little girl in the world, not that I'm biased or anything." Brooklyn paused, studied Axel's face—read the judgment in his heart—and scoffed. "No, she's not home alone while I'm out drinking, jerk. She's been asleep for hours. Her usual bedtime hits about an hour before the time I get home from this Kindred thing, so my sister is staying with us this week, until I get my check, to help babysit. She loves her aunt, so she's actually been having a great time."

"Sorry, I didn't think... ah... I got you." Axel muttered.

"C'mon, it's hard enough being a broke single mom without getting judged for getting drinks with somebody for the first time in, like, two years."

Axel gazed into his beer. She wasn't wrong about his discomfort with this, but she had misread his reasoning. It wasn't her getting drinks tonight that bothered him, but rather, her doing Kindred's death trial. *Still, not like I can judge. At least her kid is alive. More than I can say.*

And with the shitty lifestyle I lead, who the hell am I to judge anybody, whatsoever? "So, uh. Well…" He took another drink. "You were talking about the psych screening, and whether it's real or not. Gotta admit, Brooklyn, pretty sure the only reason I got into this program is that I lied like hell."

"Maybe you did, but I didn't," she answered, visibly relieved that he had moved on from the previous topic. "But even if I had, my public record alone should've locked me out of something like this. Back when I was a teenager, I tried to kill myself four times, and my parents sent me to a psych unit for it. Almost burned it down once too. I've got court records all over the place. Vandalism, shoplifting, whatever. Back when my ex-boyfriend was punching the fuck out of me every night —" She pointed at her anisocoria eyes. "— I called the cops over and over, even if they never did anything, just to make sure he had a paper trail. Meanwhile, I've got abuse records from my parents, from my ex, some other exes… so tell me, why the hell did Kindred select me, out of fuck even knows how many applicants, as a safe person to inject with their little death potion? Hell, man. I never expected that they would accept *me*. On the first day, I almost didn't go, because I started wondering if it'd be a scam."

Her tone was so intense that Axel felt the urge to back away, but he didn't. *She needs support. People haven't been there for her. Be there. Be different.* "I'm sorry," he said, feeling increasingly protective of her.

"For what?" she asked.

"Stuff that happened to you."

She laughed. "You have nothing to do with it, obviously, but I appreciate that. Hell, you're actually being awesome, listening to me go on about this. Back at the trailer park I live in, or at my old job, none of my neighbors act like I exist, you know?" She stared into her glass. "If I died, nobody would care."

"You exist. And I'd care."

"Thanks. Nice thing to say to somebody you just met." Brooklyn smiled. She gazed into his soul for a moment, and Axel forced himself not to break eye contact. He couldn't stop himself from seeing the wrinkles under her eyes, as well as the tiny strands of gray hair, and realizing that she was going to die someday. *Permanently. She'll climb that tree. Everyone will.* Even though death was an obvious reality that he'd always accepted in the back of his mind, his recent experiences with the afterlife—or the mid-afterlife, whatever it may be—had made such thoughts harder to ignore.

He finished his glass then signaled to the bartender for another. Brooklyn gulped down the rest of hers on cue. "So." Axel exhaled. "Probably should talk about the Stranger."

"Oh, man, was that the scariest goddamn thing ever or what?" She shuddered.

Axel laughed. Somehow, as horrifying as it all was, having someone to talk to made it all feel better. Even Brooklyn's profanities—which had gotten increasingly excessive with every drink—made him feel more comfortable. Meanwhile, the bartender hadn't noticed them, so Axel signaled for her again.

Brooklyn shifted closer to him. "So, whose face did you see on the Stranger's mask?"

Axel bit the inside of his cheek. *Maybe not that comfortable, actually.*

"Tell me. Please." She nudged him. "Okay, fine, I'll rephrase this, because I have a sneaking suspicion about how this 'Stranger' thing works. Be straight with me—when you applied to Kindred, you wanted to see somebody. A dead somebody. You wanted to talk to them again, and that person, I bet, is your Stranger. Who was it?"

Axel bristled away from her. "Making assumptions."

"Don't bullshit me. Nobody signs up to have a bunch of wacko doctors kill them every day, again and again, unless they have some dead loved ones they want to talk to in the afterlife. Deathscape. Whatever." She exhaled annoyedly. "Fine, here's mine. I wanted to talk to my dead boyfriend, okay? Not the fucker who hit me, but a different guy. Daniel. The father of my daughter."

Axel tried to take a drink, forgetting his glass was empty. "What was he like?"

"Nicest guy ever. Really, *really* nice." Brooklyn smiled, and for a moment, the purity of her expression was a glimpse at the person she could've been if the world hadn't beaten her down. "We tried to get pregnant for a while. Didn't happen. We miscarried twice. Then one day, we do get pregnant. Poof! Total accident. Happiest eight months of my life... aside from pregnancy itself being a total drag, anyway. And then one day, he goes fishing... hold on." She wiped her eyes. Her voice was getting choked up. "Stupid asshole goes on a fishing trip with his buddies, like he does every month, and winds up dead. Drowned. Just one day my life's on the right track, the next—boom! It's over. And I have this kid. Beautiful girl, Gwendolyn, the best of the best. But at least once a week, she looks at the pictures of Daniel on the wall, and she asks me what her dad was like. Every day, I have to see the emptiness in her life, not having him there, while seeing so much of him in her. It sucks. Fucking sucks."

Brooklyn moved closer to him. He put his arm around her. His heart ached, knowing exactly what her daughter—*Gwendolyn, she said that was her name*—was going through, having a parent she'd never know. *And the pressure on Brooklyn has gotta be immense. Single mother. Can't even imagine.*

The bartender finally arrived. "Sorry it took so long for me to get here. Had an issue with some broken glass." She wiped sweat from her brow. "Can I get you guys another round?"

Brooklyn wiped her eyes, laughing through her tears. "Yeah. A hundred percent. Sorry, I forgot your name, it's... hold on, I've got it, your name is—"

"Hoshi," the bartender answered. She had a nose ring, dimpled cheeks, pink-dyed hair, and a meager smirk that made it clear she was too sober for drunken small talk. "Same beers this time?"

"Hoshi," Brooklyn leaned over the bar. "I've got a loaded question for you. How do you feel about death?"

"Um, awkward?" Hoshi laughed. "I guess I hope it doesn't happen to me tonight? That'd suck."

"I'm being serious. My friend here has some thoughts." Brooklyn nudged him, and Axel buried his head like a shy second grader. *Not talking about this with a bartender. Is she crazy?* "Axel doesn't say much, but he told me earlier how it's weird to think how everyone in history, everyone in this room, everyone you know, they're all going to experience this dark, deep thing. And we never really talk about it aloud, it you know? But at the same time, we *always* think about it. It's the most mysterious life milestone of all life milestones. All your dead family members did it. All the living ones will, someday. It's wild."

Hoshi nodded, glancing back toward the other customers. "Weird to think about, for sure."

"Hoshi, what do you think happens after death? I guess that's what I'm asking."

Hoshi poured new drinks for them both. Axel remained quiet. *Not into the idea of talking to Hoshi right now.* He was surprised when Hoshi answered Brooklyn's question. "I don't know, really," the bartender said. "I don't think anybody knows. My aunt died last year —"

"Sorry to hear it," Axel said. *Okay, guess I'm talking to Hoshi.*

"No sweat," Hoshi replied. "Her whole life, that lady was so sure that something great was waiting for her on the other side. Then, she was actually dying, and she was scared as hell about it. Kinda strange to see it happen." Hoshi sighed. "Since then, I've been thinking. Even if there is some sweet afterlife, or reincarnation, any of that, it's gotta involve some loss of who you are, right? After you die, you stop being *you*,

I think, and you just become a part of some bigger whole thing. Kinda scary."

"Yeah." Axel gulped. *Climbing the tree. Joining The Everything, as Shoshana put it. Hoshi knows more than she realizes.*

The old couple on the other side of the bar beckoned Hoshi over for new drinks. She signaled that she'd be right there, then turned back to Brooklyn. "Thanks for asking," she said, with surprising genuineness. "Feels good to talk about it. Anyway, you guys set?" she asked, and when they gestured affirmatively, she left them.

Axel took a swig of his new beer, fearfully realizing that after everything Brooklyn had revealed to him, it was almost his turn to unspool. "So," he said, breathing heavily. "In your death, the Stranger was wearing Daniel's face."

Brooklyn nodded as she took a drink. "You bet. And who was your Stranger?"

Axel took another drink. *Tell her.* He inhaled deeply. *She told you her truth. Tell her yours.* "My son."

"Shit." She touched his shoulder. "That sucks, dude. I thought it was going to be some people you shot in the military or something."

"Nah. Anything that happened overseas haunts me, but it feels... there's some weird disconnect. Like there was a different person in my body. I can't explain it." He shook his head. "But I don't feel any disconnect from the fact that I killed my son. And my wife."

Brooklyn's mouth opened, but words didn't come out. "Wait, you don't mean..." Her eyes became fearful.

"I don't mean like that," Axel muttered. "It was an accident. But still my fault. Idiot that I am."

"How... how did..." She drank again. "Axel, I don't know what to say. How did it happen?"

Axel stared into the mirror behind the bar, and for a moment, he saw Shoshana staring at him, right in the eyes. *Tell her,* he heard her say in his mind. *Let it out. You haven't talked to anyone. Not even Malik.*

Everybody needs to talk. "My wife..." he almost froze up then continued. "Shoshana was her name. Loved her like crazy, but I screwed up everything we had. Got so overwhelmed with work, life, just being depressed about... shit, I don't even remember what I was depressed about. But I stopped talking to her. We just became strangers. She wanted me to open up. I didn't. You keep that divide going long enough, it kills anything that's good in a relationship." He looked into Brooklyn's sympathetic eyes. "You can imagine what a pain in the ass I am about not opening up, usually."

Brooklyn held him. "You're opening up now. Keep talking."

"Yeah... yeah." He nodded. *She's right.* "First, we argued a bunch. Then stopped talking. It just went like that, until one day, she told me she needed to..." Axel held back tears. "To take a break. Separation. She had a sister in Florida, so she said that maybe she and the kid should go there for the winter, y'know, spend some time thinking about whether we had a future together or not. The thing is..."

Axel's teeth clenched. His heart pounded in a combination of rage and existential dread. Brooklyn shifted away from him in fear, and he relaxed. Then she hugged him and said, "It's okay. I'm here."

"The thing is that it was supposed to be a bluff. She didn't *want* to go. She kept begging me to tell her to stay." He exhaled. "Subtle hints at first. Then just outright saying it. Not subtle. And I couldn't. I would just... stare at her. Stare and say nothing. Pretty soon, her bluff turned into a reality, because I pushed her into it, by not doing a goddamn thing to save our relationship. I just let it wither. She didn't get tickets until a week before she was supposed to go, and even then, I didn't stop it. I even drove her and Aaron to the airport. As I was dropping them off, Shosh told me—real straight, real direct—that if I asked her to stay, she would. I couldn't do it. So stupid." He took another deep breath, wiping away tears. "Then Aaron, he asked me to go with them. To either go with them, or they could stay with me. He knew something was up. And I told him... that I couldn't go."

Axel's heart was racing. He felt as if he was reliving it. Brooklyn hadn't let go of him, and as more tears rolled down his cheeks, he continued. "Well. Remember that hurricane that roughed up Florida last year?"

"Oh, God," Brooklyn whispered.

"Yeah. They got swept away in that. I saw it on the news, didn't even think about it, because I usually never pay attention to the weather in Florida, until... I don't know. The realization just hit me—that they were out there. I spent the whole fucking night calling Shosh's phone. She didn't answer. Kept hearing her voicemail, thinking it was her answering, knowing it wasn't. Because I knew they were dead. Washed away. I just knew it. Tried to call her sis, but she was dead too." His voice was choked up, and he squeezed his fists. "And if I'd gone, maybe I could've done something... or maybe I should've told them not to go. Either way, if I'd done *something*, things could've been different."

"I'm so sorry, Axel." She hugged him. "That's awful, man. But it's not your fault. The hurricane—you didn't cause that."

"Whatever." He drank the rest of his beer, and he hunched forward. They sat in silence, and Axel could vaguely hear her reassuring him, but he didn't care. He knew it wasn't okay. *It's my fault, no matter what she says.* He again looked into the mirror behind the bar, and Shoshana was staring at him with a tearful expression. He covered his face. *Don't think about it.* He breathed in, breathed out, and suddenly realized that Brooklyn had been talking to him. *I gotta stop zoning out that way. Rude as hell.* "Hey," Brooklyn said, snapping her fingers in front of his eyes. "Axel Rivers, are you still here on planet Earth?"

"Think so." He lowered his head, doing a half shrug. "My bad."

"Sorry, I know that was a lot to put out there. I appreciate it, seriously I do. But did you hear what I said?"

"Nah." *Might as well admit it.*

"I have to go. I just got a text from my sister. My daughter woke up, and she can't get back to sleep. Keeps asking for Mommy. She can't pick me up without also bringing Gwen, and if she does that, Gwen will *never* go to sleep. Can you please walk me home?"

Axel wanted to say no. *Should be an easy answer, right there.* Brooklyn was pulling things out of him that scared him. The idea of drawing even closer to her, and her life—and her daughter, Gwendolyn—terrified him. But it probably wasn't safe for her to walk that far, drunk, alone. He didn't want to make her call up her sister for a ride, either. *Going with her is the right thing to do. The responsible thing to do.* And despite his strong desire to start distancing himself from this new friend—an instinct stemming entirely from fear—the conversation they'd just shared made the deeper connection between them impossible to walk away from.

"Yeah." He finished his drink and took out his wallet. "Let's go."

Chapter 10: Homecoming

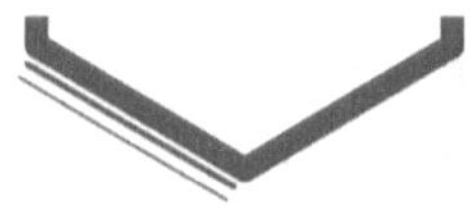

"Tell me right now to stay, and I will," Shoshana said with tears in her eyes.

Axel stood outside his car—he'd left it running—and Shoshana and Aaron were before him, waiting for him to change the situation. They were at the airport. Cars were honking, because he hadn't pulled over properly. It was almost too late to save things, and Axel couldn't figure out what to do.

"Tell me, Axel," Shoshana pleaded. She took her glasses off to rub the tears from her eyes.

Axel stood there like a mannequin, barely able to make eye contact with the woman he had devoted his life to. He loved her. He wanted her to stay. He didn't know why he couldn't just tell her that. On some level, he knew that it was because he didn't want her to feel forced. He didn't want his desires—his wants—to drag her deeper into his own personal mess. On a deeper level, though, he was afraid of hurting her. Because all along, from the moment they'd met, he'd always thought Shoshana deserved better than him, and his own inaction to save their relationship felt like the ultimate proof of that.

He gazed at her sneakers, remembering the day she'd bought them. They'd had an argument that day. One of the last arguments he'd actually participated in, instead of just clamming up. He cleared his throat, and said, "I don't know what to do."

"Tell me to stay," she repeated.

"Maybe you gotta go to Florida though. Might be good for us." He feigned a smile and mussed up Aaron's hair. "We need some time. Then we'll be ready to talk."

"Seriously?" Shoshana wiped her eyes. "I'm always ready to talk. Will you be ready then? Or is this just your way of kicking the can down the road again?"

"Yeah. I'll be ready then, I mean." He felt blank. Unfeeling. He knew he was destroying his life, ruining his family, but he felt helpless to stop himself. Instead, he bent down and looked Aaron in the eyes. The little boy was crying, and he desperately hugged his father. "Please, Daddy, come with us," Aaron sobbed. "Please. Please."

"It'll be —"

"Or we can stay with you." Aaron looked back at his mother, who was also crying. "Either way. I don't want to be away from you, Daddy, not even for a month. Please?"

Axel hugged Aaron tightly. He kissed his cheek. But he didn't say anything. And he'd never forget the hurt look in Aaron's eyes as the father that boy idolized completely failed him for the last time.

AXEL HAD NEVER HAD any problem with trailer parks, in general. But he knew—with the gut-level instincts of a foster kid whose life experience made him traumatically aware of socioeconomic realities—that there were good ones and bad ones. And the trailer park that Brooklyn called home, with its broken windows, piles of raccoon-ravaged trash bags on the lawn, and a scarred wooden bench with hundreds of cigarette butts wedged between the cracks, fell into the latter category. The energy surrounding the lot sliced through visitors like a dull blade—far too used up to cut smoothly, but perhaps even more painful because of it.

Brooklyn was clearly embarrassed to bring him there, but a tiny undercurrent of excitement in her voice—"Thanks again for walking me," she'd said at least three times—showed just how much she appreciated their talk that night. She gripped tightly onto his arm as they passed by a trailer that shuddered from the furious argument within, as a man and woman screamed at each other in the sorts of voices that leave permanent scars on a relationship. Axel tried not to listen too closely. Even hearing them felt voyeuristic.

Brooklyn's trailer, with its multicolored Christmas lights in the window and cutesy flowered doormat, stood out immediately as the good egg in a spoiled carton. Behind the trailer was parked a rusty old pickup truck—*her sister's truck, I guess*—and a little wooden porch next to a patch of grass. "Here we go." Brooklyn jingled her keys, dropped them, and picked them up. "Home sweet home."

They went up the back porch. Brooklyn unlocked the door, and before it was fully open, a tiny voice cried out from within. "Mommy!"

Axel did a double take, suddenly all too aware that he hadn't spent any time around a child since his son's death. *Stay calm, don't make the kid feel weird.* He felt dizzy with trepidation. When he regained his senses, he saw that the dark-haired little girl, Gwendolyn, had leapt into her mother's arms and seized her in the sort of all-limbed tight tug that children only give to the adults they love the most. "I couldn't sleep, Mommy," Gwendolyn said. "I needed you." The mother and daughter squeezed one another, locked in their loving parental embrace. Axel stood in the doorway, feeling like he had become the local ghost that haunted the trailer park—unwanted and uncomfortable. *It's hard to see this.* He looked away, exhaling. *I shouldn't be here. I guess I walked her home, so I just need to wait a second, make some excuse, and get the hell out of here.*

"I'm here, baby." Brooklyn kissed her daughter's head.

Gwendolyn climbed down. She was clad in footie pajamas. She pointed at Axel. "Who's that?" she asked, in a tiny voice so adorable that it almost brought tears to Axel's eyes.

He cast his gaze downward. *Fuck.* He tried to block out the feelings of immediate affection and protectiveness he felt for the child. *Can't do this.* Right as he was about to mumble an answer, Brooklyn nudged him. "Oh, this is Axel." She laughed. "He's a very nice man, even though he's quiet. He walked Mommy home today, so I wouldn't have to go alone in the dark."

"Hi, Axel!" Gwendolyn giggled.

"Hey."

He tried to pull back, to keep distance, but suddenly, Gwendolyn was standing before him, looking upward with a beautifully pure, innocent, and unblinking expression of curiosity. Unlike so many adults, she was unafraid of him. There was no judgment, no discomfort, just friendly curiosity. With startling confidence, the little girl looped both of her tiny hands around his fingers, and she dragged him inside against his will. "Come with me," she said. "I like meeting new people."

"Heh." Axel smiled, pushing back tears. "You sure about that?"

She frowned for a moment as if thinking. Then, she nodded. "Yeah, I'm sure. C'mon, Axel. I need to show you something."

Axel looked at Brooklyn, and she laughed. "Go for it, man," she said.

Then, despite Axel's best efforts to stay close to the door, Gwendolyn pulled him across the living room. Beside an antique-looking lamp and beneath the Christmas lights in the window, the little girl sat Axel in front of a large, baby-blue dollhouse. Lots of little plastic people populated its rooms, each of them with happy expressions. "Axel, play with me," Gwendolyn said, plopping herself in front of the playhouse. "Please?"

Axel laughed, and he looked back at Brooklyn. "You've got one self-assured little kid. No shyness whatsoever."

"Yeah, it's kinda intimidating, to be honest." Brooklyn grinned. "And this is her when she's tired, too. She has so many friends at school it's ridiculous. Her dad was like that, too."

Axel smiled at this and then turned his full attention to Gwendolyn. Despite the sharp trepidations rippling through him, he scooched down in front of the playhouse. It felt oddly natural to be around a little kid again. *As if The Bad Day never happened.* "So, uh… what kinda folks live in this house, Gwen?"

"This is Mr. Bill and Mrs. Bill." Gwendolyn pointed out two little figures, and she took them in her hands and walked them to the little dollhouse's porch. "They're very nice people, just like you. Hey, guys, say hi to my new friend, Axel," she giggled and then in an even higher voice, said, "Hi Axel!"

"Hey there, Mr. and Mrs. Bill," Axel said.

"Now." Gwendolyn handed him another figurine, quite assuredly, which had overalls and a baseball cap. "You're going to be Mr. Robert. He lives next door but comes over to the house all the time, because he's nice and helps fix things. Like the sink. Things like that. Okay?"

"Gotcha." Axel took the Mr. Robert figure and went along with her scenario. Gwendolyn continued describing the life and activities of all her little people. At one point, Axel eyed the kitchen, where Brooklyn was talking to a woman who looked very similar to her but more weathered and with shorter, lighter hair. *Gotta be her sister.* At one point, both women looked at Axel with a smile, and he waved back. He briefly pondered whether he should go over and introduce himself, but as a parent himself, he figured that it was more helpful for him to play with Gwendolyn for a little while longer, until the two sisters caught up.

Gwendolyn pulled him back into the game. "Mr. Robert, you're very nice," she said in a squeaky voice, holding Mr. Bill. "Thank you for fixing my car! I'm so glad the wheels aren't going to fall off anymore."

She pushed a toy car into him. "No prob," he muttered, laughing. And then, as Gwendolyn continued moving all her toys around the house, she sat in Axel's lap. Her tiny form nestled against his shoulder. She hummed to herself, taking his hands and directing them as far as how to play. Axel's smile pulled deeper into his cheeks.

"You are nice," Gwendolyn said from his lap, arching her head all the way back, upside-down, to look at him.

"Thanks." Axel choked up. "You're... nice too, Gwen."

He held her as they played with the house together—a child without a father and a father without a child. Axel laughed with her. His heart felt warm as the little girl pulled him deeper and deeper into her game. And as he played, before the watching eyes of Brooklyn and her sister, it took him a moment to realize that tears were rolling down his cheeks. Oddly, crying felt good.

AFTER THE DOLLHOUSE game started repeating itself over and over, Axel said he was tired—"Oh man, Gwen, I think I need to lay down and get some sleep, what about you?"—and while Gwendolyn seemed dubious of this, she did go to her mother. After some a brief protest, Brooklyn brought her down the hall to her bedroom to read her a bedtime book.

"Bye, Axel!" Gwendolyn cried out from the hallway.

Right before she disappeared, Axel waved back to her. "See ya, kid. Thanks for the fun game."

Axel spotted his reflection in the TV screen across the room—sitting crisscrossed on the living room floor, smiling like a fool, eyes puffy with tears—and he promptly stood up. He chuckled. *So ridiculous.* He took a moment to walk around Brooklyn's trailer, hoping to get a better sense of who she was. The worn-out, ancient furniture either came from a thrift store or was passed down by somebody's grandparents. Fifteen-year-old concert tickets were tacked to a corkboard in the hallway, alongside other young adult memorabilia such as a bottle opener from a local brewery, a high school hall pass covered in signatures, and a yellowed postcard from the Bahamas.

There were a number of cheap multi-picture frames tacked up on the walls of the living room, and it was pretty easy to pick out Daniel. Even if his beaming, extraverted grin hadn't been the spitting image of Gwendolyn's, the fact that the guy appeared in at least half the photos made it obvious. *Looks like a good dude, though. I can believe he treated her well.* One particular photograph of a far younger-looking Brooklyn and Daniel kissing on top of a mountain had fingerprints on the glass. *Brooklyn never moved on from him,* Axel thought. *Definitely can understand that. Truth is, I probably never will, either.*

Clearing his throat, and wiping any residual tears from his cheeks, he stepped into the narrow kitchen. He filled a glass with tap water. *Gwendolyn and Aaron would've really liked hanging out with each other,* he realized, feeling weirdly comforted at the thought. *With how shy Aaron was, and how bold Gwen is. Would've clicked well.*

"You're good with kids," Brooklyn's sister said.

Axel jumped. *Forgot she was here.* "Uh. Thanks."

Outside the window, the neighbors were shouting violently again. The sister glanced outside, frowned, and then redirected her attention to Axel. "I'm Cindy," she said, and Axel couldn't help but notice how much older Cindy looked than Brooklyn. The lines on her face pulled downward, and her eyes were harder—but no less intense. "If you walked Brooklyn home, you must have signed up for that same sleep study thing that she's doing this week?"

Axel paused before speaking. *Weird. Guess Brooklyn is giving people the same bullshit excuse that I told Malik.* "Yeah. Name's Axel Rivers."

She shook his hand. "Nice to meet you, Axel." Her palms were callused and cracked, with bruises under her nails—clearly, the hands of someone who did manual labor for a living. "I'm guessing," she said, "that you must be the guy Brooklyn talked about last night. She kept saying you were cute. Not sure why."

Axel smiled. "Oh yeah?"

"Oh yeah. At least, that's what she thinks," Cindy said, eyeing him carefully—intrigued but not trusting. "You a vet?"

"Yeah. You too?"

"Army."

"Funny how we always recognize each other."

"Well, you know what they say about eating enough dirt." Cindy grinned from the side of her mouth. "No matter where or how you eat it, all dirt tastes the same."

They both laughed. Cindy then glanced down the hall where Brooklyn and Gwendolyn had gone. "Hey, I don't want to be all over-protective big sister or anything, and I don't know what you and Brooklyn are doing, but... well, be careful with her, okay?" Cindy pushed him—gently but firmly. "She's had a hard life. Lots of awful things happened to her, and the last guy..." She shook her head. "You seem a lot nicer, but I don't make good assumptions about anybody until I see evidence. Maybe there's nothing happening between you too, or maybe there is, and that's your business, but be careful with her. Or I'll beat your ass, Axel. I swear."

Axel nodded. *This is getting weird. I didn't even plan to come here. I'm not dating her sister. I don't even know if Brooklyn likes me... or, well, I guess she does. Does she?* "She's a good person," he said.

"She is."

"Been through some shit, that's for sure. I promise not to hurt her. And..." He paused, considered, and said his true thoughts. "I respect you taking care of her like this. Telling it like it is. She's lucky to have you."

Cindy was visibly intrigued by this, but before she could say anything, Brooklyn returned from the hall with a wistful smile on her face. "Aaaaand she's asleep!"

She does look beautiful, Axel thought, surprising himself. *Different than before.* Seeing her as a gentle, protective mother, it became apparent how much he'd misjudged her earlier, or at least, made assumptions without seeing the full picture. She was still the hard-drinking, hard-swearing person he'd drunk with, but she was something else, too. *Everybody's complicated, I guess. No matter how hard we try to be simple.*

Catching Cindy's suspicious glance, Axel realized he was staring a bit too hard at Brooklyn. Brooklyn noticed, too, and smiled at him.

Brooklyn got another beer out of the fridge. "Want one?" she asked Axel. He shook his head politely. Turning to Cindy, Brooklyn said. "Gwen just needed some Mommy time." She popped open her beer. "Cindy, thanks so much for staying here this week. I don't know what I'd do without you. I hope Naomi doesn't mind." She turned to Axel as she took her first drink. "Naomi's her wife."

Axel nodded. "Cool."

"Well, duh, I'm here for you," Cindy replied. "And hell, with those late shifts Naomi's been working at the nursing home, we haven't seen each other all that much these last few months, anyway. But seriously, no problem."

"Thank you," Brooklyn said. "Hey, question. Gwendolyn begged me to drive her to school tomorrow. Can I borrow your truck? I'll have to leave crazy early to get her there and then make it back here so I can catch the bus to—" She eyed Axel. "Y'know, our sleep study. But it'd be really nice to get some time together, with how little I've gotten to see her the last couple days. Would it be okay?"

Cindy laughed. "Hey, if it means I get to sleep in tomorrow, I'm down. Drive that kid to school."

The two sisters talked for a moment. Axel sipped on his water. *I should go. They have something good here... family, connection. I'm just getting in the way of that.* He put his glass down and cleared his throat. "Glad you got her in bed okay," Axel said, shifting between both feet. "I should, ah... get going. Get some sleep."

Cindy narrowed her eyes. "Didn't you just spend all day sleeping? For that sleep study?"

"Yeah, well. Still tired." Axel yawned. "Thanks for everything."

"You don't have to head home, y'know." Brooklyn smiled from one side of her mouth. "You could stay here, Battle-ax."

Axel shifted uncomfortably. *I could.* He knew, deep down, it could be a good thing. For her, and for him. He saw that taking that step could be a building block to a future. However, Shoshana's face kept popping up in his mind. *Drowning. Her and Aaron.* He envisioned them in the hurricane, calling for him—and then he thought about the Stranger and knew that he couldn't stay. *I need to focus. Get up early, get to Kindred. Confront the Stranger once and for all.*

"Nah. Thanks, I just..." He gestured toward Gwendolyn's room, as his eyes welled up again. "I should go."

Brooklyn touched his hand, and she put her beer down. "No problem. I'll walk you outside."

"Thanks for getting my sister home safely," Cindy said.

"Sure."

Brooklyn guided Axel to the door. "Let's go," she said.

Axel shivered as she walked him outside and back onto the little porch. A cold breeze rustled through them, and Brooklyn moved closer to him. They stepped down the porch steps, one by one. She sat down on the little patch of grass behind the trailer, gently pulling Axel—who was now trembling so hard he could barely breathe—down with her. She stared up at the full moon. "Beautiful," she said.

Axel inhaled deeply. "You are."

She smiled and whispered, "*You* are."

Axel rested his shaking hands in his lap. Brooklyn inched even closer to him. "I'm sorry about everything you've been through," she said softly. "It's awful that you had to go through that. But thanks for being there with me tonight, after everything that we... well, whatever we went through today at Kindred. I don't know how I'd be doing right now if I hadn't gotten to talk to you tonight."

"Appreciate it. You were there for me, too. Really meant a lot." Axel said. Then he stared up at the night sky and sighed. "Crazy, looking up at this, isn't it? Thinking about how much is out there, you know? After dying, especially. Seeing that massive tree that holds up the universe. It's wild." He shook his head. "We're such a small part of something so huge. Infinite."

"Sure, it's infinite, but..." She paused to squint upward then shrugged. "On the other hand, big machines don't run unless all the little pieces work, right? And infinity... we might be small, Axel, but y'know, maybe we're still totally vital to the whole thing running. Every decision we make influences every other part of it, I think. Even after we die. Might as well make the most of it while we're still alive, I say."

Axel thought of the Deathweavers. "Yeah. Maybe —"

Brooklyn kissed him. At first, Axel fearfully held himself firm to the ground, but when she kissed him again, he softened into her embrace. She rolled on top of him, gently pushing him to the grass, and they kissed a third time, then over and over. She softly bit his lip. Their cold bodies entangled with one another, beneath the glow of the stars and moon. Axel ran his hands down her back, and as she pressed her body into his—eliciting a shiver through them both—an inner warmth spread outward. *This feels good.* They hugged each other tightly. *It feels right.*

Finally, Brooklyn pulled back, looked at Axel with a beaming grin, and she whispered, "Okay, that was nice." Then she stood up, kissed him one more time on the cheek, and walked back up her porch. "Thank you, Axel. See you tomorrow, okay?"

Axel smiled. "Yeah, see you tomorrow."

Chapter 11: Unlife After Undeath

After Axel and Shoshana slept together for the second time, he woke up at 3:00 a.m. from nightmares. Memories. Memories of overseas. Memories of a dead man's dead eyes. He jolted upright, drenched in sweat, feeling the dull, empty sting of isolation that had greeted him so many times. But this time, a gentle hand stroked his back, and he didn't feel so alone.

"Hey," Shoshana whispered. "Are you okay?"

His heart steadied. He felt safe. Wanted. He glanced back into her concerned eyes, and he lay back down beside her. "Yeah," he said, running his fingers through her tangled black hair. "That happens to me a lot. Nightmares like that. Stuff I saw when I was in the military, a lot of the time. Sometimes it's stuff from childhood. The car crash that killed my parents. Little sensory details from that, like the blood on the cracked windshield, always get stuck into other things. Had nightmares my whole life, but they just seem to get worse every year."

"I'm here," she said, kissing his stubbly cheek. "I want you to know that you're safe with me, because I feel safe with you. I know I can't fix the nightmares, but anytime you have one—whether I'm here or not, just call me. Seriously. No matter the time."

Axel smiled. He kissed her. He wasn't sure what it was, but something felt so different about the connection they had, compared to past relationships. It felt right. He looked at the bedside clock, seeing the early hour. "Hey," he said, "How do you feel about the idea that we get up right now?"

She laughed. "To be honest, Axel, I'm not thrilled. But I'm listening."

"I'll make you a coffee. We'll go up the road, all the way up that big hill, and we'll watch the sunrise over the water. How about it?"

Shoshana stretched her arms, with a wide but tired grin. "Okay, just because it's you. As I said, though, I'm not thrilled, so this better not become a habit. And that better be a really, really strong coffee you're preparing. Promise?"

"Promise."

They hurried out of bed. Axel threw on some clothes, started the coffee pot, then ran back to make sure Shoshana was getting up. She wasn't—in fact, she'd already fallen back asleep, so he woke her up again, helped her get dressed, and walked her to the kitchen. "Coffee," he said, handing it to her. "Drink up."

Then, hot beverages in hand, they started the car. As it warmed up, and the fog lifted from the windshield, they smiled at each other. Minutes later, they drove up to the top of the big hill, and waited together, until the clouds turned pink, and a glorious new sun painted a glowing streak across the water. As the darkness lifted, they clasped hands. The nightmare was gone. The road ahead looked the brightest that Axel had ever seen it. And without thinking—without doubt, hesitance, or concern—he kissed the woman beside him, feeling thankful on a level he couldn't express in words.

"I like hanging out with you, Shosh," Axel said. "You do make me feel safe."

"Wait, 'Shosh?' Okay." Shoshana laughed, and he leaned into him. "Forget that attempted nickname, please. But I like hanging out with you, too. Let's keep doing it."

AXEL FELT SO GOOD AFTER leaving Brooklyn's place that he wondered if something was wrong with him. He caught himself randomly smiling a few times, and the realization of this only made him smile more. He didn't know what the future held, but for the first time since The Bad Day, this uncertainty didn't terrify him.

Downtown was quieter than usual. Half of the bars had finished their last call, and the ones still open were full of the usual mix of old townies and college kids. A small crowd of people were laughing outside of the small place before the bridge, Barfly Heaven, which had a chalkboard out front proclaiming that it was open mic night. Axel was surprised to feel companionship in the people outside, rather than aversion. *Me, feeling good about something. About people. Been a while.* For a minute, he considered going in, having a drink, and borrowing someone's guitar to play a song or two, but quickly changed his mind. *Don't get crazy, now. Just let the happiness sit with you for a little while.*

He crossed the bridge and left downtown. He stopped at the sign for Sunrise Circle, a small community of lakefront houses. Back when he'd still been driving, he'd used to drive his car through the circle, every now and again, and admire the lavish properties there. This past year, he'd ditched that habit, just like he'd ditched a lot of things, but tonight felt different. He touched his lips, remembering the softness of Brooklyn's kiss, and he gazed up at the treetops, imagining their limbs stretching out across the sky, spreading the essence of his lost loved ones back into the universe.

"Well," he said aloud, with a still-buzzed half-smile. "I just died twice. Probably should do something I like."

Axel cut right into Sunset Circle, and walked along the waterfront, as starry reflections tingled across the surface of the lake. The architecture in this community had always fascinated him, with its rustic A-frame cabins perched a few houses down from modern gray cubes. All of these lake houses, he knew, were far beyond anything he'd ever be able to afford. Most of them weren't even living residences, but seasonal rentals, which spent much of the year being empty. Still, passing by all of them had often given him hope of a future where he could bring

Shoshana and Aaron to such a house, if only for a few nights, just like his parents had done for a younger Axel so long ago.

He stopped at a smaller house, a log cabin, with a slightly rundown appearance but a glorious, massive porch. *This one feels accessible. Like maybe we could've afforded it, for a night.* Standing at the edge of its slanted driveway, gazing downward, there was a small rocky beach. He closed his eyes, smelled the water, and whispered, "You would've loved this, Aaron." Then, he thought of Gwendolyn, and smiling to himself, he imagined surprising Brooklyn, her sister, her sister's wife, and the little girl with the gift of a night's rental at this house. He didn't have to go with them—his presence didn't matter. But he wanted them, particularly Gwendolyn, to have a chance to make good memories there.

After checking that there were no cars in the driveway, he crept downward, and he glanced in the windows. *Empty. It's an unoccupied rental. Out of season. Perfect.* Then, he swung open the gate to the porch, walked up to the edge, and leaned forward. The cold night air, the sound of the lake, the trees in the distance, all cascaded around him in a way that felt unreal. *I can't believe how good this feels.* He'd gotten so used to feeling empty that feeling full—full of vitality, new experiences, and ideas—was exciting. *What if this is the beginning of something? Maybe.* It felt risky to even ponder that possibility, but he was open to it. After spending so long closed down, maybe it was time to reopen. To call Malik and tell him everything. To see Brooklyn again. To get a new job, a good job, once this Kindred experiment ran its course. *First, though, I have to die a few more times. I have to see Shosh again. To help whatever part of Aaron is trapped as the Stranger.*

Footsteps crunched behind him.

He turned around in shock, expecting to find an angry landlord or renter. No one was there. At first, he wrote this off as his imagination. *Just me creeping myself out. Just like how I can't sit with a door behind me, all that other junk.*

The boards of the porch creaked. He flipped to look. No one was there. But when he stared back into the windows of the house, he did see a reflection of a hooded figure in place of his own. The phantom's face was cloaked in shadow. Its hand was mangled. "Ah, shit," Axel whispered, as his heart stopped.

He closed his eyes, reopened them, and his ordinary reflection had returned. He left the porch. The magic of his night had died. The time for sentimentality was over. He had to get home, get some sleep, and be ready for Kindred in the morning.

THE WALK HOME WASN'T peaceful.

Axel was being followed. That, he knew. He wasn't sure whether the creature following him was a hallucination or a real embodiment of what he'd seen in the Deathscape, but real or not, it was on the prowl. And the more he walked, the louder its footsteps became. Everywhere he went, rushing from suburban blocks past multiple apartment complexes, it stayed close behind him, but just out of sight.

As he got closer to home, the sound of footsteps was accompanied by whispers. Whenever he turned around, though, nothing was there. Tension ratcheted up inside him, but he had nowhere to put it, so he put his emotions aside, snapped into his old military mindset, and trudged ahead robotically. He just kept walking. *Tomorrow,* he told himself. *I'll fix things with the Stranger... with Aaron, when I die again tomorrow. I'll make sure that whatever part of Aaron this is, I give it the opportunity to climb that damn tree and be free. Whether he needs to forgive me or beat me down, I'll do what I gotta do.*

By the time he reached his own apartment building, he was drowsy enough that he could almost drop in place and fall asleep. *Just a little further. Gotta rest. Gotta get up in the morning.* Crossing the parking lot, he smelled gasoline emanating from his neighbor's car. *Ah, Old*

Joe. C'mon, man, you gotta get that fixed. Not safe. Joe's leak had worsened since last week. He peered underneath. A rainbow-reflected puddle had settled around the tires. *Maybe I'll just fix it for the guy after all this Kindred shit is done. Tell him he can just pay me with a six-pack, or whatever. I'm not working, so I definitely got the time.*

A shadow fell over the car. He turned around. The Stranger stood behind him, as real as the asphalt beneath their feet. Blood dripped down its mangled hand.

Axel stumbled backward, colliding with Joe's car. "Aaron, I'm sorry." The Stranger didn't reply. It walked beneath the streetlamp, and yellow light cascaded off its plastic Aaron-styled mask. The crack down the center of the mask had worsened, becoming charred, and the mask was pulled tight into a monstrous smile.

"Aaron," Axel cried out, "we can talk —"

The Stranger reached out for him with its mutilated hand. Axel took it into his own. "I'm here for you, kid," he said.

The plastic mask smiled wider, revealing razored teeth. It squeezed Axel's hand. The flesh of Axel's fingers fused to that of the Stranger. The burning sensation was white-hot. Smoke spewed into the air. The stench of burnt flesh rose into Axel's nostrils. Hot blood – no, not blood, melting skin – dripped from their melted appendages.

"Let go!" Axel tried to pull away.

The Stranger's plasticized mouth grinned further and further up the sides of its head, extending past the eyes and into the forehead. The smoke darkened, blanketing the world and leaving nothing but the Stranger's face. Axel yanked and pulled, harder and harder, but his hand was still fused to the Stranger and wouldn't come free.

"I'm sorry, Aaron!" he shouted, but the apparition would not listen. A throaty gurgle emerged from its throat, as it pulled Axel closer. Suddenly, Axel felt a million hooks in his back – tiny, razor-sharp ones – and he realized that countless fishing lines of light were hooked into him, connected to the physical world. *Parts of me,* he thought. *Parts of me connected to everything else.* As the Stranger brought him closer to it, each of these hooks was ripped out of him. He was separated from the cosmos. Severed from the Great Tree.

Axel roared out in shock, and in the blackness of the smoke—as the outside world disappeared—his body was rushed forward, jammed into the shape of the Stranger, and then draped in a dark hood. "No, I can't," he sputtered, before his lips fused together.

A plastic mask, much like the one the Stranger wore, floated over his head. Its visage was not of Aaron, though, but of Ax Rivers—the child version of Axel, crying in agony as his parents died. Tears rolled down Axel's cheeks. Blood dripped down his back. And the Stranger, with its increasingly awful smile, slammed the plastic mask onto Axel's face, and pressed it onto his skull with jagged nails.

THE SMOKE LIFTED. AXEL found himself sprawled out beneath Old Joe's car, his clothes soaked in gasoline. He jumped up, startled, but the Stranger had faded into the shadows. His hands hurt, but there were no signs of injury.

A streak of blood pooled in the gasoline. His forehead stung. He frantically felt his face, then his forehead, only to find a tiny cut on his temple. Thankfully, there was no mask and no nails.

He'd hallucinated the whole encounter. That made sense. Unlike his trips to the Deathscape—which still felt painfully vivid when he woke up—his earthly experience with the Stranger already was fading, much like a dream does. *So, it wasn't real. Just a reaction to Kindred's treatment. I imagined it.*

Somehow, that didn't make him feel any better.

AT 3:00 A.M., AXEL stormed inside his apartment. He'd spent nearly thirty minutes hunting the parking lot—and the surrounding neighborhood—for the Stranger, to no avail. *Because I hallucinated all of that, so of course I couldn't find him. What a waste of time. I need to confront him in the Deathscape, not my own damn brain.* He raced to his door, panting with exhaustion, and dug into his pocket for his keys. By the time he finally got them out, he was shaking so frenetically that he dropped them. "Fucking goddamn it..."

As he reached for the keys, his vision blurred, and for a moment, he could've sworn that he saw the keys become tangled in the white tendrils of one of those strange Deathscape flowers. He blinked. *Nothing there.* The keys were just on the hallway carpet. *Get to sleep, man. A few hours at least.* He unlocked the door, swinging it open way too aggressively, and slammed it shut behind him.

The lights were on. He heard creaking behind him. He raced toward his bedroom to get his gun, only to hear a sigh from the living room.

It wasn't the Stranger, or somebody breaking in. It was just Malik, sleeping on the couch. As Axel hovered over Malik, his eyes opened and he drowsily rubbed his face. "Axel?" He yawned. "God, man. I waited for you to get here... what time is it? Geez."

Axel stumbled over to the window. He fearfully peeked between the blinds to look out at the parking lot, somehow more terrified of the Stranger's absence than the possibility of seeing it again. After a moment of tense breathing, he sat across from Malik. "Sorry," Axel said. "I didn't know you were here. Freaked me out."

Malik yawned again and sat upright. "No shit? I've been texting and calling you all night. Was worried something happened to you, man. Do you even have your phone on you?"

Axel reached into his pocket. His phone was dead. "Forgot to charge it."

"Are you okay, Axel? What the hell were you doing? Just drinking by yourself or something?"

"Drinking," Axel muttered, staring into his dead phone. "Not by myself. With a friend. I'm okay, Malik. Thanks for —"

"Hell no, you're *not* okay," Malik said, frowning. "Stop with the bullshit, man. I've known you since we were kids, and I know when you're lying. And, hold on..." He leaned closer. "What's with that blood on your forehead? You get in a fight or something?"

"Sorry." Axel crumbled his face into his hands. "Nah, I fell in the parking lot. Drunk. Stupid mistake. But I'm all good, man, just let me go to bed."

"*Talk* to me, Ax." Malik got up and stood next to him. "For Christ's sake, dude. I've told you a million times. What happened to Aaron and Shoshana is not your fault. It just isn't. Stop punishing yourself. You can't keep this up. You need to..."

Malik's words became a blur. *So tired.* Axel couldn't look at him. *He doesn't understand.* "Have to sleep," Axel muttered. "Have to get to the... the clinical trial. Tomorrow. Few hours from now." And with that, Axel rose up, stumbled down the hallway—bypassing a protesting Malik—and collapsed into bed.

AXEL IS DREAMING. HE'S not dead. But some part of him is still locked in the Deathscape—he feels it, the weight and reality of it—and he wonders if maybe dreaming itself is just another temporary gateway to that strange place.

He is climbing up the Great Tree. "I'm coming!" he cries out to all of the fragments of souls awaiting his arrival. His fingernails dig into the bark. He seizes branches, yanking himself upward. Every push hurts. Every muscle aches. Sweat rolls down his back. He looks down to track his climbing progress.

The Stranger climbs right behind him.

Axel continues climbing. His teeth are clenched. His hands slip on a slick plastic surface—and he scrambles to regain his balance. Looking up, he sees that a giant blue sign has been nailed to the tree, blocking his path, and it says KINDRED ETERNAL SOLUTIONS in glowing letters.

As Axel slips, he desperately clings to the sign's edges, hanging from it in midair. It flickers pink, then blue, then blue again. Security cameras swivel from its sides. "Why are you here?" Axel asks, pulling himself to face the cameras. "How can you scar something so perfect with a stupid goddamn corporate logo?"

The Stranger seizes his leg. Axel's grip slips. The Stranger pulls him loose, and with one mighty swing, Axel is thrown down to the abyss. Down, down, down he falls, through new galaxies and black holes, faster and faster, until the Stranger—and the Kindred sign—are now just tiny specks above him.

"Brooklyn!" he cries out, but he doesn't know why. In the darkness, as if responding to his cry, Brooklyn and Gwendolyn appear. Mother and daughter, together. But they aren't happy to see him, and as they start to speak, the flesh of their faces become mottled. Their eyes drop out, leaving empty eye sockets, and their bodies crumple into piles of flesh.

Axel's fall is broken when he crashes into cold water.

BY THE TIME AXEL WOKE up, the midmorning sun was already casting long shadows across the bedroom.

"Shit!" he jolted upright. *I'm late.*

Beams of sunlight pierced through his skull, giving him a throbbing headache. He forced his way through the tangled blanket and out of the bed like a creaky and rusted piece of machinery, then rushed to the living room. Malik was still sleeping on the couch, the morning was well underway, and the clock on the microwave said 9:11 a.m.

Axel's saliva ran warm. He rushed to the wastebasket, just in time to fill it with vomit. His ribcage leapt upward, trying to jam itself through his neck, over and over, until the vomiting finally ceased. Only slightly less creakily than before, he stood up. The clock now said 9:22. *I'm so late. They're going to kick me out. And then...* He panicked. *If I get kicked out, I can't confront the Stranger. I can't apologize to him. I'll never be able to... never...*

"Stupid idiot. Dumbass!" Axel grabbed his dead phone along with a charging cable, pocketed his keys, and rushed out the door.

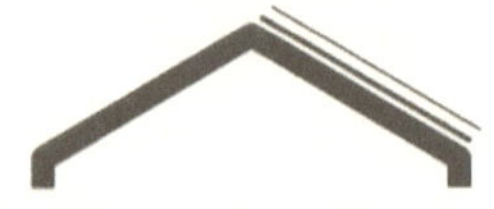

Chapter 12: Turning Point

Axel had sold his car six months ago. He'd hated to do it, but the sale had helped him bite a decent chunk out of his badly expired debt sandwich. Besides, since The Bad Day, he rarely went anywhere, and he lived only a block away from the grocery store, so the vehicle had mostly been sitting in the parking lot. In all that time, he'd never regretted the decision to go carless—until that morning.

The bus had left hours ago. Between an empty wallet and the sky-rocketing rate of taxis, all Axel could do was pound the pavement by foot. Dried out, dehydrated, with a splitting headache and gelatinous legs, he raced mile after mile until finally, panting, he reached the Kindred office building. *I've gotta convince them to let me stay.* He paused, heaving with nausea, begging his legs not to drop him to the ground now that he'd finally made it. *Have to make it okay to Aaron. Have to die again. Have to.*

It was early afternoon. His fellow test subjects had died hours ago.

He lurched through the front doors and swayed down the corridor on uneven feet. Kindred's lobby was empty, except for the same receptionist he'd spoken to two days ago, who was still hiding away behind her bulletproof glass. At the sight of Axel—unwashed, hungover, and no doubt reeking of desperation—her chair slid backward, as if even the glass wasn't enough to protect her. "Can I help you, sir?" she asked.

"Trial. Death trial." He panted. "Ah, I mean, I'm late. Really late."

"Oh. Can I get your name?"

"Rivers. Axel."

She put her glasses on and scrolled through her computer. "Yes, I see. I'm sorry, Mr. Rivers, but today's session is halfway over. You were a no-call, no-show today—it says here that you have been removed from the program."

"Wait, please —"

She raised a hand, refusing to face him. "This was clearly written in your contract, Mr. Rivers. Top of the second page."

"I need to —"

"You will receive no payment," she continued, "and we expect no further discussion on the matter. Understand that if you break the NDA, you will be brought to court. As a courtesy, Kindred will permit you to wait out front for the night bus, if you wish, so you have transport back to town. Have a nice day."

HOURS PASSED. NIGHT fell. And Axel Rivers, no longer a paid volunteer for Kindred Eternal Solutions, waited outside the building. Not for the bus ride—he didn't care about that, at this point—but only because he wanted to see Brooklyn when she was resurrected again. *To make sure she knows why I won't be here anymore. That I'm not leaving because of her.*

Axel felt numbed to the realities of what had occurred. Earlier in the day, he'd flipped out in the lobby—going so far as to punch a soda machine—but after being escorted out by security, he'd done nothing more than stand out front, lost in his own misery. As the hours had dragged on, he'd entertained thoughts of breaking in and giving himself one last dose—*I just need to see the Stranger one more time*—but the practicalities of this seemed too high a barrier. *Even if I jabbed that formula into myself, what if they didn't resurrect me?* Considering they were already docking all his pay after killing him twice, it didn't seem hard to believe. After all, a live lab rat who gets kicked out might squeak to somebody, but a dead one can't break an NDA.

The more he thought about it, the more he wanted to see Brooklyn. *Maybe I could send a message to the afterlife through her. Have her talk to her Stranger, and maybe try to have hers find mine... somehow. Maybe that's asking too much.* He glanced at the doors of the building. The test subjects were finally starting to exit, with the same paled skin and nauseous poses as the previous days. *Still. Maybe it's an idea. I can ask her.*

Axel stood like a statue, letting the resurrected people from the building pass on either side, sometimes bumping into him as they recovered from their third delirious experience. Some of them were crying. Others were expressionless. All of them looked like walking corpses. He waited, eyeing each person, trying to spot the woman who had kissed him beneath the stars just one night ago.

He didn't see her. "Brooklyn?" His lip trembled.

The test subjects continued to stumble past him, barely registering his presence. More and more of them walked past, and he stared at every face. Some of them had blue eyes. Some of them had black hair. None of them were Brooklyn. He waited. He waited until the last person came wandering out the doors, and even then, he kept waiting.

Brooklyn wasn't there.

BENEATH THE LIGHT OF the full moon, Axel's shadow fell over Brooklyn's trailer park. It looked and sounded much like it had the night before. The next-door neighbors were shouting at each other again, as if their previous argument had gone on uninterrupted. As Axel's heels ground through the gravel, though—and he wiped the sweat from his brow, somehow still pushing through a fatigue that had never lessened since that morning—he felt certain, deep in his heart, that she wasn't going to be there. *Maybe she slept in like I did,* he told himself, but somehow, he didn't believe it. He'd repeated this over and over in his mind the whole walk, as his stomach felt sicker and sicker. The other voice inside him—the darker, more sinister one that had once told him his wife and son were dead in Florida, only to be horribly validated by the bad news—was spouting the same messages now. *Don't listen. She's gotta be okay.*

A sedan was parked, still running, beside Brooklyn's trailer. Its tail-lights cast a red glow against the other trailer behind it, and the person at the steering wheel was masked by tinted windows.

Axel stopped. *That's not Cindy's. She drives a pickup truck, right? Yeah.* He crept forward. The Christmas lights in the windows of the trailer suddenly went dark. The back door swung open. He sprinted forward, begging to any higher power that might be listening—any god, anything in the Everything, even the Stranger itself—that he would see Brooklyn's blue eyes and know that she was okay.

Instead, he nearly crashed face-first into Cindy. "Holy shit!" Cindy cried out. "Axel, what the hell are you doing here?"

Axel wobbled backward. "Cindy. I mean, Brooklyn. I'm trying to find Brooklyn." He leaned forward, supporting his weight on his knees. "She wasn't at the, ah, our thing today. I couldn't find her." He swallowed. "Needed to make sure she's okay."

Cindy's eyes were red and damp. She was wearing a mechanic's coveralls, and a half-unzipped backpack, with a cellphone charger peeking out, was slung over her shoulder. "Damn it, Axel." She rubbed her eyes. "I'm sorry."

"What the hell does that mean?" Axel pointed at the car. "Who the fuck is —"

"It's my coworker. He gave me a ride because my car... Brooklyn... oh, God." Cindy choked back tears. She took hold of Axel's shoulder. "Brooklyn's dead, Axel."

Axel could barely take in her words. He felt as if he were sliding out of his skin. "Shut up. No."

"Yeah, she's dead."

"Nope." Axel shook his head frenetically. He backed away from Cindy, rejecting her attempts to reach out and hug him. "Fuck that, Cindy." *Can't be true. The bad voice can't be right again.* His gaze shot to the small patch of grass where he and Brooklyn had kissed the night before. "She can't be dead." He frantically tried to keep his voice from cracking as words thoughtlessly spilled out of his throat. "Can't. Unless you mean in the, ah, the sleep study. We die every day. In the study. She can't really be dead. She's just in the Deathscape. Not dead. Can't be dead." His eyes stung. He rubbed them. *Don't cry. If you cry, it means she's really dead. Don't let yourself cry.*

"I get it... it's..." Cindy touched his arm. He jerked away. She kept talking, her voice increasingly choked up. "She drove Gwendolyn to school this morning, in my truck. Somebody... I don't know, she got sideswiped by somebody who was driving drunk. Other driver is dead too. Both cars totaled." Cindy straightened her shoulders, clearly trying to push back the emotions pouring through her voice—and when she spoke again, her demeanor became distant and locked up in a manner that reminded Axel of himself. "She died instantly. I got called while I was at work. But I gotta go. I'm heading back to the hospital now, because Gwendolyn—"

No. "Please tell me she's okay."

"No. Sorry." More tears broke through Cindy's resolve. "Gwendolyn's in the ICU. They're doing everything they can, but they don't think she'll make it more than a few days. They basically have her on life support. I just came here to get my stuff so I can stay at the hospital tonight, in case she... she..." She wiped her eyes. "My wife, Naomi, is there now, staying with her while I'm running back here, but I've gotta be there too. I have to."

Axel clenched his fists. *Calm. Stay calm.* "Cindy, I'm sorry."

"I don't... don't... I don't know what to do." Cindy couldn't stop herself from sputtering. "Axel, I feel so helpless. My sister is dead. I tried to protect her, I... she's gone, Axel... oh my God."

Axel hugged her. She hugged him back. They gripped each other in the cold, trying to process it all. "I can't believe she's gone," Cindy whispered. "I can't lose Gwendolyn too. Gwendolyn is the only part of Brooklyn I have left."

Axel swallowed the lump in his throat. Over Cindy's shoulder, he again stared at the patch of grass then at the stars, knowing he'd never look at them again without thinking of Brooklyn, and hating that fact. *She can't be dead.* He closed his eyes. *Has to be a mistake.* He remembered her smile and the way she'd made him feel, if only for one night, like there might be a future worth living. *And she's dead now. Dead, stuck with the fucking Stranger, unless she's already climbed the tree. She wasn't ready. It's so unfair that Gwendolyn has to grow up without a mom, unless she also...*

He tried not to let himself think about what came next, but based on Cindy's description, the writing was on the wall. *Unless Gwen dies, too.* He thought about the sweet girl who had shown him her playhouse the night before. *The girl who wasn't scared of me.* He thought about her innocence. How genuine she'd been. He straightened himself, pushed back tears, and took Cindy's bag over his shoulder. "Here," he said, "let me get this for you." He placed it in the waiting sedan's open trunk.

"Thanks," Cindy said. "I'll let you know, if you just give me a number, or —"

"Nah." He exhaled. "I want to go with you."

Cindy hugged herself. "Okay. Let's go."

AXEL STOOD ALONE IN the waiting room, watching a bland infomercial on the TV screen. He felt separated from everything that was happening. Stranded. But he didn't know what else to do, so he waited.

Cindy and Naomi had gone to be with Gwendolyn again, but Axel—as much as he'd wanted to be there—found it too hard to be in the girl's presence. *Triggering. Guess that's the word.* Seeing her there in a hospital bed, connected to so much machinery, had brought back such a flood of memories that he felt like Aaron and Shoshana were dying all over again. His pain had roared back, like a fire rekindling itself in the ashes. He'd known that if he stayed in the room any longer, he would've had a meltdown, and the situation would've become about him. He didn't want that. He wanted every minute—every second—to only be about Gwendolyn right now.

The informercial ended. Another one took its place. Axel paced back and forth, barely paying attention, just wanting someone to bust in through the door and tell him that the little girl was going to make it out alive.

Internal bleeding, he thought, remembering what the doctor had said. *Punctured lung. Broken bones. Burns. No brain damage detected so far.* He hated the thought of her in pain. Hated the idea that her life had reached such a devastating exclamation point at such a young age. *She's going to die, though. You know that. Cindy knows it.* He brushed back tears. *And Brooklyn's already dead. Permanently dead.*

Axel sat down in the corner of the room, where his phone was charging, and turned it on. Once it booted up, he searched for Brooklyn on social media and scrolled through her various profiles, resumes, looking for some sort of relief that he couldn't quite place. Most of her posts were cute puppy memes, inspirational quotes, or—to his surprise—group photos with friends. He refreshed the page, and noticed a slew of comments from these friends, each of them expressing shock and sadness at her death. Axel analyzed every word. *She had all these people who cared about her*, he thought, considering how the only person left in his own life was Malik. *And even if she had friends, a sister, a daughter, she still died. It didn't matter.* He searched for her in the local news. A photograph of Cindy's totaled truck was posted right beneath a headline about a single mother dying in the crash. He winced. The broken windows in the back seat, where Gwendolyn had certainly been sitting, were hard to look at, as well as the blood on the cracked windshield.

He put his phone down, shook his head, and got up to make himself a cup of coffee. Mostly, he did this because he couldn't keep still, as opposed to any desire to drink it. *C'mon, Gwen, pull through this.* Just as he was mixing in cream and sugar, Cindy rounded the corner, with eyes just as puffy as Axel's. "Hey," she said.

"Hey." Axel passed her the coffee he'd made. "Take this. If you want it."

"Thanks. I was one hundred percent about to make one, so..." She slouched against the wall and sighed.

"Is she... uh..."

"The same as before." Cindy sipped her coffee. "No changes. The doctors certainly aren't very hopeful, either. They won't outright say she's going to die, but you know... if you read between the lines and know how to speak their language, they're saying it. You know what I mean?" She swallowed back more tears. "I don't know. Don't know how I even feel."

Axel stared at her, feeling the words she wouldn't say. *You're scared, like I was. Blaming yourself, like I did. Like I'm doing now. You're telling yourself you shouldn't have loaned her the truck that morning. I'm telling myself I should've spent the night. Maybe if I had done that, it all could've been avoided.* Axel thought of all this, but he sensed that Cindy was a person like him, who felt awkward about being analyzed—*the opposite of Brooklyn in so many ways*, he thought painfully—so all he said was, "I know what you mean."

"Thanks for being here," Cindy said. "It means a lot, especially because... I don't want to sound rude, but you barely know us. Me. Gwendolyn. Hell, you barely knew Brooklyn."

Axel shrugged. "Connections run deep sometimes. Even if they're new." Then, after a pause, he forced himself to say more. "I lost my wife and kid a year back. Haven't had a real conversation with anyone since then, until Brooklyn and I met the other day. She was a special person. And Gwendolyn's a good kid. Just want her to be okay."

Cindy's mouth slipped to the side, and she looked at him with unexpected empathy. "I'm sorry. That's awful that you had to go through something like that."

"It is what it is. Listen, Cindy, tell me if there's anything I can do. Anything at all."

"Appreciate that, but... Axel, unless you've got some direct line to tell God, the Grim Reaper, or whoever's controlling this shit, and you can tell them to spare Gwendolyn's life?" Cindy scoffed. "Yeah, otherwise, not much you can do. But thanks."

Axel frowned. *Well, maybe I do.* He trembled, trying not to show the course of action that was coming together rapidly inside him. *Maybe.* "I need to sit down," he muttered. "I might have an idea."

He sat back in the corner. He rubbed his eyes with shaky hands. Cindy sat beside him. "Whoa, are you okay?"

Newfound purpose shot through him, refreshing his batteries. *Don't know the Grim Reaper. But I do know the Deathweavers. If I died again, if I talked to them...* He eyed the exit. *Even if there's no way back for me, I could do this.* He stood up. "Yeah, I'm going to try something. Gotta go. Keep me updated."

"Wait —"

Axel marched out of the hospital.

AXEL SAT IN HIS APARTMENT with the lights off and the gun in his hands.

This isn't like the other times.

Back when he'd done this before, four times over the past year, there'd never been much deliberation involved. Holding the gun in his mouth or to his head had been—in a way he didn't like admitting—a source of comfort. When he felt the trigger under his finger, he knew that if the pain ever cut too deep, if the future ever seemed even a smidgen more painful, he could pull it and be released.

This wasn't comforting anymore. Not just because what came after death was no longer quite as uncertain as before, but also because this time, there wasn't just deliberation. There was a plan.

He started to lift the gun. His chest seized up with tension. He dropped it. *Shit.*

I have to do this. He picked it up again. *I have to save Gwen.* He knew his plan wasn't foolproof, but it was the only one he had. If he could break free from the living world and reenter the Deathscape, then it stood to reason that he could find the Deathweavers again. *Talk to them. Convince them.* Even though they had ignored him last time, he felt certain that if he pushed against them with everything he had, or at least made a convincing argument, they could spare Gwendolyn's life—as long as he got to them before she died.

Unless they just ignore me. In which case I'll die for nothing.

He switched the gun from hand to hand. It felt heavier than usual. He stared at the streetlight outside the window, and he sighed. *C'mon. Have to save Gwen. This is the only way.* He remembered her innocent smile. *Have to.* He thought of Brooklyn. He thought of Shoshana and Aaron, his parents, and Malik. His eyes felt empty of tears, but despite his best efforts, he couldn't put the gun in his mouth. His heart was racing.

Can't go on like this. Decade after decade. Knowing that if I'd done it, I could've maybe saved that little girl's life.

Axel raised the gun. He felt the trigger. *Put it in your mouth. Get it over with.* He couldn't do it. He closed his eyes, tried again, and his phone buzzed. "Shit," he muttered. He dropped the gun to the floor, looked at his phone, and saw that it was Malik.

He'll find out I did this here tonight. As he called. Axel stared at Malik's photo on the phone. *He'll blame himself. I can't ignore him.* He answered. "Hey."

"Hey, are you okay?" Malik sounded terrified. "Wow, you actually answered. So good to hear your voice, man.

Axel rubbed his eyes. "Good to hear yours, too."

"What was going on last night?"

"It was a shitshow. This sleep study is, ah, it's brutal. I'm sorry you had to see that. But look, Malik, I have to go."

"Are you okay, Axel?" Malik's voice was choked up. "Please, man, I love you. You're the only brother I ever had. I can't afford to lose you, and if there's anything else I can do to be there, man, I will. I swear. Just talk to me. Tell me."

Axel looked at the gun on the floor with a heavy heart. He remembered the first time he'd met Malik in school—a smiling kid, a foster kid like him, the first person he'd ever met who actually understood. He closed his eyes. "I've got some issues going on, Malik," Axel said.

A relieved sigh came from the other line. "Finally, an admission."

"Yeah. Last night was rough. But I love you too, Malik. I have to go right now, because there's something serious, ah, I have something I need to do. To help someone."

"You're not bullshitting me, right?"

Axel smirked. "Nah."

"Okay. Call me tomorrow, okay?"

"Will do. Bye."

Axel hung up. *At least I was honest with him. Even if I die, that means something.* As he stared back at the gun on the floor, though, resignation set in. He didn't want to pick it up. He didn't want to die.

He stood up, stretched, and tried to calm himself. His heart kept pounding. *Has to be another way to save Gwen without offing myself. Has to.*

He stepped out onto the porch. Instantly, he became overwhelmed with an icy chill that he hadn't felt when he was outside before. "The hell?" He crossed his arms. A high-pitched whine rang through his ears. He squinted in pain. *It's here.* He stared down into the parking lot.

The Stranger stared up at him through the empty holes of its mask. Axel froze with terror. *Stay calm.*

"I'm coming your way," he whispered. "Somehow."

The Stranger nodded, clearly unintimidated by this threat. *It hears me. If it's real.* Its black robes rustled in the tailwinds of the cars. The crack in the center of its plastic mask was, once again, deeper than before. Darker. The plastic cheeks, with their plastic tears, were charred and burnt. Axel's stomach clenched. He didn't look away. "Or you could just take me with you right now, Aaron," he said. "We can talk. And then you can bring me to the Deathweavers."

The Stranger shook its head. The creature's mask twisted, forcing Aaron's plasticized face into a sinister smile. It stepped backward into the shadows. Axel leaned hard against the railing. *I'll go down there. I'll make it happen.* "I'll find a way," Axel said, "even if I have to break into Kindred."

He paused. *Wait. There's an idea.*

The Stranger had vanished. Axel breathed heavily. *I don't need to break into Kindred. Just need to find someone with access.* He thought about Dr. Kendra Carpenter, remembering the note he'd seen in her office. *I think it said her address was 888A Fifth Street.* He knew that if he tracked the woman down to her house like a lunatic, she might very easily call the cops on him. However, as he plugged the address into his phone, he also knew that this was his best chance—his only chance—of saving Gwen without losing himself.

Dr. Carpenter's place was a thirty-seven-minute walk. He had no time to waste.

Chapter 13: Displaced Broken Bones

888 A Fifth Street was one-half of a downtown duplex. The lights were off. No car was in the driveway. Axel's knocks on the door had been answered only by the mewing of a gray cat, and after waiting for another twenty minutes, the same feline had taken to peering out at him from the kitchen window with hostile yellow eyes. Clearly, the tenant—Dr. Kendra Carpenter—was not home.

Maybe she's getting drinks with coworkers. Axel sat on the doorstep. *Or has a partner. Or is drinking by herself. Who the hell knows? I barely know this woman. She could just as easily be working late or sitting alone at the lake.* He had no other leads to follow, so he waited, trying to forget just how suspicious it was for him to be turning up at her house in this manner, and hoping that she wasn't sane enough to kick him out the second she did turn up.

He sighed. *This is the only way to die temporarily again. Only way to talk to the Deathweavers and save Gwen's life.* He watched the ticking clock on his phone, each minute ratcheting up the tension, as he envisioned wisps of life sliding from the little girl's fingers. *C'mon, Kendra. Get home. Let's do this.*

Sick of waiting, Axel checked the time. He felt confident that Gwendolyn hadn't died yet, but just in case, he called Cindy.

"Hi, Axel," she answered. Her voice made it clear that she'd been crying again. He hesitated before replying.

He swallowed. "She's okay, right?

"She's still here."

He closed his eyes tightly. *Wow, what a relief.* "Okay. Okay. I just had to check. Has anything changed?"

"One sec." Cindy's voice became muffled, as she talked to Naomi for a moment. "No, it doesn't seem like anything has changed at this point, from when we last spoke to the doctor. Not anything that I understand, anyway. Are you heading back here or...?"

He gnawed his lower lip. He wanted to tell her the truth, and to explain his plan, but he knew that the second that he, a stranger, starting saying weird terms like Deathweaver and Great Tree, she would no longer allow him to visit them in the hospital. *It just sounds so out there unless you've been there. But God, I hate to lie to her.* "I'm still working on something," he said, finally. "Trying to get in contact with somebody who can help."

"Huh." Cindy sounded extremely dubious. It made him feel bad, even though he didn't blame her. "Let me know if you find this person or figure anything out, then."

"Will do. Keep me in the loop, okay?" He paused. He wanted to say, *let me know if her status changes and I'll rush over*, but he knew that if his plan did work, and he was dead, rushing over wouldn't be possible. So, instead, he said, "Take care."

He got off the phone, lightly tapped it against his knee, and went back to waiting for Dr. Carpenter to appear. Another ten minutes passed. *Malik once said that if you want to get somebody to show up, just give up and do something else. Might as well try it.* Thinking fondly on this, he got up and circled the building.

In the back, a small, grassy backyard, surrounded by a chain-link fence, was shared between both sides of the duplex, each half separated only by the long, dark shadow he cast from beneath the streetlamp. It took him a minute to place which side was Dr. Carpenter's, but when he did, he saw that her back door had been left slightly ajar. He tightly gripped the chain-link fence, and considered how easy it would be to climb over it and open her door. *Maybe I could do it that way?* He let go. *Nah. Don't even think about it.* Shaking his head, he started to walk away—then stopped. *What if she has the death serum right in there though? Hell, it could be on her kitchen table. Or not. Why the hell would I assume she brings that nasty stuff home with her?*

He stared at the open back door, then back at the road. The thought of breaking in and looking for that death serum, practical or not, seemed so much easier than waiting around for her to appear. He knew what it looked like, after all. He could find somewhere safe to inject himself. Get it done. After envisioning this whole scenario, though, he shook his head. *What a stupid damn idea. Even if you break in, and even if you don't get the cops called on you, and even if you manage to miraculously find and inject yourself with the serum—if it's even there—nobody'll be there to wake you up.*

This last point, he realized, was the clincher, and with a heavy sigh, he walked away. He returned to the front driveway just in time to meet the blueish headlights of a shiny new electric coupe. He couldn't see the driver, but he felt confident that it was her, so he braced himself. *Get ready. Talk normally. Don't act weird, because she's already going to be freaked out about her patient being here.*

The door swung open. Dr. Carpenter exited the vehicle, her short gray hair shining yellow in the streetlight. Her ear was cocked to her shoulder, with a cell phone tucked between. She hadn't noticed Axel. "Jen, I know," she said, laughing. "We haven't seen each other in so very long." She emerged with an array of grocery bags clutched between reddened fingers. "Well, Jen, I should go. I just got home and —"

At the sight of Axel, Dr. Carpenter's eyes popped from their sockets. She dropped her bags. A carton of eggs broke open. Fragmented eggshells and yolk splattered onto the ground. Her phone crashed into the same puddle.

She faced him in horrified silence, her mouth ajar. "Why the hell are *you* here?"

"Uh, hey," Axel said.

"Mr. Rivers, it's... I'm not..." The humor and kindness she'd offered him at Kindred was no longer evident. Axel's enormous shadow fell over her, and he felt her cringing away from him. He stepped back, lowering his shoulders, trying to seem smaller, as she reached into her purse. "I have money," she cried. "Whatever you need. Please, just don't —"

"Nah, hold on." Axel lifted his hands up. "Doctor, I just —"

"Don't hurt me."

"I just need you to kill me." Axel said, as calmly and rationally as possible. "Please."

Her eyes, shining white in the darkness, softened. "Pardon?"

"I know this sounds crazy, but listen. There's a little girl out there. Gonna die tonight." Axel exhaled deeply. "I got kicked from the program. Signed up for it because... well, none of that matters, but doctor, I need you to kill me and bring me back one more time. Because me going back to the Deathscape is the only chance this girl's got."

"Mr. Rivers, that would be completely unprofessional." Her tone was startlingly businesslike. "And how do you possibly believe you can bring someone *else* back? That would be unprecedented."

Axel took a leap of faith. "Because I saw the Deathweavers," he said. *Please know what they are.* "I think I can talk to them." *White lie.*

Dr. Carpenter froze. "Stop right there." She wrinkled her brow in astonishment. "You made... contact?"

"Yeah." *Please, please listen to me.* "Need to talk to them again. Only chance of Gwen... this little girl, I'm her only chance. Have to make a deal of some sort, and working with you is my only way of getting back in there unless I kill myself. I don't want to kill myself, Doctor. But if I have to... if I have to..." He stood up, pacing down the driveway. *She can't understand.* "I already lost my kid. My wife. Everything. I just want to make something right. My son, he should be... shit, how old would he be..." *I don't remember.* "God." *I'm rambling. Shut up.*

Dr. Carpenter no longer seemed scared. Her keys were in her hand. "I lost my own child as well," she said, staring into her chest. "I understand that all too well. The guilt never leaves you. You never feel like yourself again."

Axel swallowed. "Nope." He noticed that she wasn't wearing a wedding band, either.

"Axel..." Dr. Carpenter sighed. "Nobody has ever come back from seeing the Deathweavers, much less made contact. The info we do have is so minimal. Well, to be fair, two people did come back from seeing them, but they became psychotic, so..." She eyed him up and down. "You don't seem psychotic. I don't know what it means that you saw them. But it certainly means something."

She scooped up what remained of her groceries. She walked right past him, toward the front door. Axel stared at her in bewilderment. "Are you saying...?"

"Your story has my heart." She unlocked her door. "But to be frank, Axel, that's not why I'm going to help you. As a scientist, I can't turn down a good opportunity to learn more about the Deathweavers. And if you've seen them once, much less had a dialogue with them, or if you do find a way to manipulate them..." She beckoned him. "Come inside."

THE FRONT DOOR OPENED into a yellow-tiled kitchen, cluttered by unwashed kitchen gadgets. "Take a seat," Dr. Carpenter said, gesturing toward the dining table, with a stern voice that was unlike anything Axel had heard from her in their previous interactions.

Axel sat down. The gray cat from the window hopped onto his lap. "Huh," he said. "You're a lot friendlier than you look." He ran his hand down the purring creature's back. Dr. Carpenter flicked on the lights, revealing that the table was covered in notebooks, textbooks, and tablets. A corkboard across the room was covered with tacked sketches of the Deathscape—the very same Deathscape Axel had been to, with the Great Tree, the Glass City, and the white flowers. "This is nuts," Axel whispered.

"Tell me about it." Dr. Carpenter took a blood pressure cuff off the wall, and she wrapped it around Axel's arm. "Welcome to stage two of Kindred's operation, by the way."

"I was kicked out." The cat jumped off him.

"Indeed." She took out a pen and a pad then tightened the cuff. "That's why we're doing this in my damn house, on my damn time, instead of in the Kindred labs. Because Kindred or no Kindred, I've spent the last two years trying to figure out what the Deathweavers are, and how to talk to them. You might be my meal ticket. If you can—hold on." She checked his pupils, pulse, and respiration, then poked at the veins on his arm. All of this she documented into her pad, with a wrinkled brow and squinted eyes. "Long story short, as long as I get the info I need, Kindred won't care how I got it. They're not exactly an ethical company, if you haven't noticed."

Axel looked at the drawings on the corkboard. "Don't know how to feel about all this."

"Well, to be quite frank with you, I don't care about your analysis of my job or my goals. But I suppose that I'm sorry to hear it makes you uncomfortable." She capped her pen. "Now, come up to my office. Lucky you, Axel, you get to learn the truth about the nightmare we've created for you people."

You people. Axel frowned. Dr. Carpenter exited the kitchen, marching to a staircase across the room. Axel took a moment to examine her apartment—the living room, he noticed, was so sparse of any decorations that it didn't even look lived in—but before he could peek at her notebooks, the doctor called down the stairs. "Follow me, please!"

He followed. The staircase wound up into a second story, where there was a bedroom and, as promised, an office. Dr. Carpenter was already sitting there, behind a massive wooden desk that had the look of a family heirloom. The kitchen had been cluttered and the living room empty, but her office looked like a hoarder's den, with literal piles of notebooks stacked as high as he was. "Welcome," she said, with a tiny undercurrent of self-consciousness that made Axel think better than to comment on anything.

More drawings of the Deathscape were tacked up all over the walls, with one in particular featuring an egg-like shape underwater. *That's the sac I broke out of.* "That's where I was," he whispered. "Or where death starts for everybody, right?"

Dr. Carpenter spun her chair to face him and pointed to a small couch across from her, beneath the window. "You'll want to sit down for this."

He did so. *This is wild.* Catching himself getting excited for a moment, he clasped his hands together and squeezed, reminding himself to stay focused on his purpose for coming here. *This is for Gwen. I don't care about Kindred's mission, Dr. Carpenter's goals, or any of that. Focus.*

Dr. Carpenter wrote something down in yet another notebook, then she sighed heavily. "So." She took off her glasses. "Let's just rewind a bit and make sure I've got all this straight. You saw the Deathweavers."

"Yep."

"Uh-huh. And you talked to them."

Axel hesitated before continuing his lie. "Yeah."

Her eyes narrowed, and she jotted something down in her notebook. "And your goal is to go back, talk to them, and try to convince them to allow some little girl—I don't remember the name you said—to live. Am I understanding this correctly?"

"Uh, yeah. Gwen."

She raised her eyebrows but kept writing. "Okay. And what about the Stranger? Have you thought about whether he's going to let you get away with it?"

Axel gazed into Dr. Carpenter's cold, clinical expression. *She knows about the Stranger. Right.* He leaned forward, gathered his voice, and said, "What the hell is the Stranger, anyway?"

"Well, not an easy question to answer. I suppose you think it's your dead son." Dr. Carpenter bit her pen, clearly uncomfortable with divulging more. After a moment, she shrugged, and visibly made the decision to let it all spill. "It's not, Axel. The Stranger is you."

Chills passed through him. "Huh?"

"In a manner of speaking, anyhow," she said. "The Stranger is a programmed embodiment of your guilt. We've coded it very carefully, based on each participant's psychological profile, to keep everyone in line... to make sure our test subjects, like you, are kept in check. The idea is that if you get too close to figuring anything out, the Stranger will force you back into our world. Jolt you back to life, if you will. That's why you generally wake up so soon after encountering it. Through fear, guilt, and intimidation." Her face took on a guilty expression for a moment, and then her eyes widened. "Hmm. Now that you mention it, *you* were the one who fought back yesterday when the Stranger program was activated. You forced your body to stay dead. That must've been around when you broke the boundaries we've set in place and found the Deathweavers. Tell me, after you came back to life, did the Stranger approach you in... well, for lack of a better term, the real world?"

Axel could barely put out words. "It did," he whispered.

"Fascinating. That doesn't normally happen, but since we implanted the Stranger into your mind, and you broke the programming by circumventing it in the Deathscape... huh." She wrote down some more notes. "What I'm saying is that tt's only logical that it would continue existing in your conscious brain, since it didn't get the chance to reboot. The program from your second death is still running in your brain, unable to turn off." She put her pen down. "I'm sorry. I'm being callous. It's just that your case is really unusual, and —"

"Hold on for one fucking second." Axel stood up. He felt dizzy. After a moment of gripping his head, he released his tension by shouting, "You programmed that goddamn thing?"

She arched away from him fearfully. He winced, forcing himself to step back. *Cool it. You're relying on her.* He stepped back again. "Again, sorry for the callous tone," Dr. Carpenter said, clearing her throat. "I suppose this whole thing is a bit alarming. This isn't about me, but I don't really know how to do something like put on pretenses or feign politeness. I'm honest to a fault, which either means I'm too friendly or I'm too direct. If we're going to work together on this, Axel, you need to know that."

"Gotcha. So you understand why I'm so damn pissed."

"I do." She shrugged. "It's just so interesting to me that it's hard to relate, but if I were in your place, I suppose I'd be livid."

Axel bit down on his anger. "Go on. Tell me more about this." He stared at the sketches of the Deathscape on the wall, avoiding eye contact with her.

"The Stranger program works, to be fair, but..." She stared out the window pensively, and then sorted some papers on her desk. "It also backfires when people occasionally push through it. You're not the first to get past it—you're just the first to do so and come out the other side with a functioning brain."

"What happened to the others?"

"Generally, if you fight the Stranger, Axel, it will disable you. Permanently, I mean." She shrugged all-too-casually. "I don't know how you accessed the Deathweavers without the Stranger killing or lobotomizing you. A fluke, I suppose."

"Can you deactivate this goddamn thing?"

"Not once you've entered Kindred's program. The Stranger is now a part of your consciousness. There's no cutting it out of you—at least, not that I know of."

Axel stood up again. *What did I sign up for?* He walked over to the window, eyeing the many lit-up windows outside, wondering how many others Kindred—and Dr. Carpenter—had tortured in this way. *So many vulnerable people, getting so messed up over a paycheck that isn't even that great. How can they do this to people?* His heart pounded so hard that he could barely breathe. "Why are you telling me all of this? There's no way Kindred allows that."

She walked around her desk and stood next to him. Her exhalations were nervously heavy. "No, it's certainly prohibited. But I'm personally in this for my own reasons, Axel. And I know that you're not going to reveal anything I tell you—because you've broken into my house." She eyed him carefully. "And that's what I'll tell the cops if I ever see you again after tonight's mission is over."

The seriousness of her threat, and the underlining racism, was clear. Still, he stood his ground. "Maybe I'll tell people anyway," he said. *Even if I get shot for it.*

"It won't matter. Nobody will believe you, and you have no proof." Her mouth became a thin line. "Kindred's PR people won't let your story become public. You'll be locked up, silenced, and nobody will ever believe the insane things you say. Sorry if that sounds hostile, but it's the truth. And that's not even mentioning the fact that unless you go through another Kindred death and resurrection—a reboot, as we call it in the lab—you'll continue to have the Stranger rattling around in your brain, stalking you in the waking world. Do you want that, Axel?"

Axel found that he was liking Dr. Carpenter less and less. However, he was also understanding her more. For all her talk of authenticity, her cold directness masked a raw pain hidden right underneath her skin. And as much as he bristled at her actions, he understood that pain all too well.

Glaring directly into her stony eyes, he said, "You said you lost a kid too. What was their name?"

She seemed startled, but she answered. "Jake." She flinched away. "Why?"

"Just wondering," Axel said. *Reminding myself that you're a human being.* "You got into this program because you wanted to talk to your own dead kid, I'll bet. Right?"

She broke eye contact. "Correct."

"Have you?"

She shook her head, crestfallen. "It doesn't work that way. At least, I haven't seen any indicators. But maybe..." She touched his shoulder. "Maybe *you* can change how all of this works tonight, if you succeed at negotiating with the Deathweavers."

Axel's stomach clenched. He pushed her hand away. He'd come to Dr. Carpenter asking for help, and now he was being blackmailed into completing an entirely different mission that only loosely linked up to his.

He sat down on the corner of her desk and clenched his hands together. *So much to take in.* "So, you mold the Stranger based on a person's psych profile," he said. He suddenly remembered Brooklyn's theory. *She knew there was something fishy about this program accepting us. She was damn right.* "That's why you pick people like me. Damaged people."

"I wouldn't say the word damaged, but —" Dr. Carpenter started, then fell back. "Well, yes, I suppose."

"Tell me more."

"Kindred does, indeed, do intensive research on every applicant. People are picked not in spite of their personal traumas, financial state, and so on, but *because* of those factors. Because..." She squirmed, clearly not wanting to say what came next. She forced it out. "If I'm going to be brutally honest, it's because Kindred wants people who are desperate, traumatized, suicidal. People who will sign their lives on a dotted line and don't have the power to fight back when we manipulate them through all of this, to reach the goal of —"

"What's the true goal?" Axel faced her. "I get the whole shit about these trillionaire assholes wanting to live forever. But there are parts of this Deathscape thing..." He closed his eyes. *The whining sound. The light. The blue Kindred signs. The Glass City.* He opened them. "Parts that don't seem right. Like they're artificial."

Dr. Carpenter pushed some papers aside to sit next to him on her desk. Axel hated how she kept moving closer to him. "I shouldn't talk about that," she said.

Axel stood up. *Hate being close to her.* "You said it yourself. No-body'll believe me anyway. I deserve to know what I'm getting into tonight. If you're gonna call yourself direct, be direct."

"I suppose you're right." She opened a notebook and closed it. "The main goal is exactly what you think, yes. Tyler, Harrington, all of them, they want to live forever. As the technology has been developed, though, a secondary goal has taken shape. The desire to... I suppose you could say put our own footprint in the Deathscape. To make our mark on this new frontier. To commercialize it, if we're going to be crass."

"The Glass City?"

"That's something we constructed. A technological marvel when you consider it. Once finished, it will be something of a tourist loca-tion, you could say... a place where the dead can go for a temporary stay before their bodies are reinvigorated and resurrected."

"If they can afford it."

She squirmed at this. "Correct. The price will be quite high. Though it'll also be a home base for researchers like myself, so we can study the Deathscape directly. And we'll need maintenance people as well, to clean up, do repairs... Perhaps you'd be interested in such a thing? It'll pay much better than this current gig you have."

Axel glared at her.

"Or perhaps you're not into the idea. Just asking." She cleared her throat. "We'll also have advertisers. Meeting rooms, so business can continue when our clients stay there. It's a whole new market. A whole new world, to, well..."

"To colonize." Axel paced across the office, shaking his head. "Motherfuckers in power never change."

"Awfully dismissive of you."

"Whatever." Axel gazed out the window then glanced back at the stairs. *I should leave. Get the hell out of here.* The thought of doing anything more to further the goals of Kindred—or even just Dr. Carpenter at this point—made him sick. The sights, sounds, and feeling of the Glass City echoed through his mind, and everything he'd heard filled him with a fierce resolve to go out and publicly reveal what he knew.

But that won't save Gwendolyn. That little girl will die unless I do something.

Axel faced Dr. Carpenter. "No more talk. Let's get this done."

AXEL LAY DOWN ON DR. Carpenter's bed. She stood above him, gowned and gloved. "Stay still," she said.

He nodded. A sharp prick jabbed the center of his arm, and fear once again raced through him. *Here it comes.* Through the open window, a gentle breeze flew inward. Behind the nearby apartment buildings, clouds passed over a moon. *Pretty,* he told himself. *Decent last sight on Earth, if this lady never wakes me up. Or if the Stranger kills me. Or if the Deathweavers just ignore me, and Gwen...*

His vision faded in and out. His heart slowed. He clenched his jaw. *Won't let them ignore me.* He knew his odds weren't great. He knew that he could very well accomplish nothing except providing further intel for Kindred to raid and ruin the afterlife. As everything slowed down, though, he stayed focused.

I won't fail you, Gwen.

He closed his eyes, losing his last moments of consciousness to a deep, utter despair. Then everything went dark, and Axel died for the third time.

Chapter 14: The Third Death of Axel Rivers

The void is overwhelming. It always is. *Stranded in Nothing. Lost in the thick of Everything. An infinity of emptiness.* This time, though, Axel knows that he can push through it all, because there is something on the other side. He knows that. Still, the fear grips him. When he's in the darkness, he feels he might never get out. That this might be it. *This is the end. Nothing comes after. No, something. Something. Something real. Something that matters. Push through. Push. Push!*

Light appears.

Sights return, followed by sounds and feelings. The cool rush of water washes over him. Axel's eyes blink. Lights flood into his corneas. The Deathscape unrolls before him like a gigantic carpet. He is standing in the rushing waters, knee deep, beneath a tangled mass of roots at the base of the Great Tree. The air is perfect. The sky glows with golden light, as the cosmos glistens behind it. Stars are born. Stars die. Black holes erupt. Planets go from cosmic dust to inhabitable rocks in space. Everything happens separately and in its own pocket of time, and yet somehow, all of it also happens at once—and together. It's too much to take in, and the marvelousness of that now excites Axel as much as it terrifies him.

I'm here, he thinks. "I exist," he says. Once again, Axel climbs onto the shores of his own spongy gray matter, no longer needing to adjust to the sights and sounds of the Deathscape. *It feels good to be back here.* He smiles. *Strange how much I've changed. How I can accept all of this, even if I sure as hell don't understand. Just had to die three times to get to this state of mind, no biggie.*

Summoning his courage to proceed, he runs his fingers through the clouds of ultraviolet mist. He approaches the nearest tree root, itself the size of a small house, and he scales it to gain a higher vantage point. Once up there, he stares outward as hills and valleys tumble before him, and somehow, deep inside, he feels—yes, *feels,* rather than sees—a pathway that he must follow.

"I'm coming, Gwen," he promises.

Coldness creeps up the back of his neck. *It's here.* He shudders. *And it's not Aaron. Not at all. Just some corporate nightmare injected into my brain. Remember that.* The horrible high-pitched whine screeches through his ears. The light of the Deathscape becomes scrambled, and when he can see again, the Stranger stands before him.

The entity raises its bloodied hand, and it points at him. A scratchy voice emerges from behind its plastic mask. Suddenly, it sounds not ethereal, but robotic. "The end awaits." It creeps closer. "For *her.*"

Axel shakes his head. *Stay calm.* He breathes in deeply. "You won't stop me from saving her."

The Stranger moves closer. Its plastic mask has split completely into two halves—on one side remains the crying face of Aaron, but the other side is now reshaped to resemble the crying face of Gwendolyn. *Damn Kindred creation trying to get under my skin. Following its programming.* Nausea spirals through Axel's stomach. His vision darkens. His veins contract. *It's trying to wake me up.* He clenches his fists.

"I'm going to the Deathweavers," Axel says.

The Stranger's empty gaze burns through him. "She's mine, Axel. Just like Aaron is mine."

Don't listen. Axel tries to maneuver away, but the Stranger follows. It raises its bloody hand toward the sky, across the landscape, and everything darkens. Axel closes his eyes. "Shoshana," he whispers. "I need you."

In the darkness behind his eyelids, a hand clasps his. He looks down, with his eyes open, but nobody is there—yet he feels her. *She's here. Finding me.* Darkness overtakes him again, and he can't see, but he still feels Shoshana's hand in his. "Please." His heart pounds. "Take me to the Deathweavers. Figured out what I need to do."

In the darkness, the Stranger looms over him, its twin masks now twisted into malicious smiles. Axel stumbles backward, as the whine of the Glass City reverberates through his skull in pulsing waves.

"Shoshana, I need you!" he cries. "Now. Now!"

A warmth overtakes him. A light. And then his body rips apart in an explosion of cosmic dust—each individual fragment housing the essence of him, and yet each separate in its own way—and scatters into the winds. The darkness brightens. He sees the Deathscape through a million eyes simultaneously as he is flown over an infinite tangle of roots, and he screams from a million mouths. He can't understand what is happening. He can't piece himself back together. Then there is a voice—a calming radiance—that recenters him.

"It's me, Axel," Shoshana whispers. "You're almost there. But you don't have much time."

IN THE CASCADE OF LIGHT, Axel hears the distinctive sound of pens on paper. He smells the ocean. *It's them.* He blinks himself back into cognizance as the individual fragments of his body flow back together into a cohesive whole. The colors, shapes, and smells of the Deathscape sink into him, slowly, until once again he finds himself standing on the same shoreline he visited before. It hasn't changed. Lined up along the expanse of the beach stand the Deathweavers, each one perfectly enmeshed in its own world, all of them charting out the course of the universe with their pens, tools, and instruments

Axel's feet crunch in the black sand. He steps forward. His legs wobble. He knows that all of his resolve has brought him to this moment. He has broken the rules. And now, his efforts will be either a success or failure.

Talk to them.

"Thank you, Shoshana," he whispers, as he marches toward the vast array of tentacled creatures spread before him.

As he draws closer to the Deathweavers, memories of his life appear in his mind's eye. The faces of every death he has faced in his life—Shoshana, Aaron, his parents, the people he saw die overseas, Brooklyn—push inward, crowding out his thoughts. *Keep walking.* The Deathweavers don't seem to notice him. Their dozens of eyes remained fixated on their many sketchbooks as their tentacles draw geometric figures and equations upon each piece of paper—hundreds of pens, simultaneously drawing out the universe.

Axel steps closer, even though every instinct within him is trying to run. *Keep going. For Gwen. Don't back down.* A white orb within the closest Deathweaver's transparent chest spreads out into the tip of its every octopus-like limb, irradiating each pen with energy. Its eyeballs are heavy and wet, but rapidly flicking from side to side, to observe a different sketchbook. And the closer he gets to the creature, the more he admires the complexities of its skin —that is, if such a substance could truly be called skin—with mysterious shapes, textures, and energies flowing down each inch of it. The Deathweaver feels bigger and bigger, while he feels smaller and smaller.

Axel comes within touching distance of the Deathweaver. It doesn't visibly register his presence. It looks between its many drawings, redrawing each of its maps. Revising, updating, rebalancing—a neverending process. Axel starts to speak, but his voice retreats into his lungs. *Damn, this is heavy.* The realization that he is about to spit out Earthling sounds to an architect of reality itself—the sheer smallness of his own existence, the audacity of what he is trying to do—is so over-whelming that he can't quite process it.

"Uh...hello?" he mumbles, feeling the most inconsequential he has ever felt in his life. The Deathweaver does not react. Axel waits for a moment. *I know it heard me.* The tentacled creature still does nothing, continuing to work on its sketchbooks, oblivious to him. It seems either unaware or indifferent to the fact that he risked life and limb to come see it.

Axel clears his throat. "Hello."

Again, the Deathweaver continues its work. Tears sting Axel's eyes. *It doesn't care.* His childhood comes leaping into his throat as he chokes back a sob. *Just like nobody ever cared when I was growing up.* He feels his whole life reverberating through him—the constant sense that he was disposable, a throwaway person, someone who didn't matter—as the tentacled being ignores his presence, proving once and for all that his deeper suspicions were always right. *It doesn't care about people like me. People like Brooklyn. It doesn't care that this little girl is going to die.* Axel lowers his head, brushing away the tears, once again feeling like the little boy whose birthdays were never celebrated, because they didn't matter. *Always a statistic. Something to pity. Always a lost cause.* He turns away from the Deathweaver, turns away from the Great Tree, and stares down at his own meaningless feet. *I don't matter. Nothing matters.* He starts to walk away.

Wait. He stands upright. *Gwendolyn matters.* He remembers the little girl who sat on his lap, showing him her dollhouse. The life, energy, and hope she brought back into his heart. Then, turning to face the sky, he remembers his son, Aaron, as a baby. He thinks about the way that he would rock Aaron to sleep and the deep, all-encompassing love the child had for him. *That matters, too. Children are treasure chests of potential. Gwen deserves a chance to live.*

Axel turns around, reapproaches the Deathweavers, and he places his foot on the creature's pad, colliding with its pen. "I'm Axel Rivers," he announces. "Here to make a trade for the life of a little kid named Gwendolyn."

For a terrifyingly long moment, the creature freezes. Its infinite work has come to a halt, each tentacle stopped in place. With painstaking concentration, each of the Deathweaver's heavy eyes turn to face Axel. For thirty seconds, Axel knows, firsthand, exactly what it feels like to be an insect staring up at the eyes of a frustrated giant.

The Deathweaver whips its tentacle out. Axel flies off his feet, face-first into the sand. The creature resumes its work.

"Damn it," he mutters. He spits out sand. *Don't let that stop you.* He scrambles back onto his feet, feeling emboldened—*it reacted to me, that's something*—and this time, he walks directly in front of the Death-weaver, blocking its view of one of its pads.

"I'm not going to let you ignore me," Axel says.

The Deathweaver's eyes blink, in what could only be disbelief. Axel glares back at it. This time, it does not fling him away. Instead, its glistening tentacles reach around him to continue their work. Before Axel can interrupt it again, a deep reverberation emerges from the creature's core. An inhuman, electrified voice shocks the air, and it says, "We know who you are." The Deathweaver glares at him, for the briefest of moments. "We know everything about you."

Each of the Deathweaver's words is pronounced wrong. The cadence is wonky. It is clearly imitating human language through an alien voice box that wasn't made for such a task. But hearing this reply, Axel's heart leaps into his throat. *You're doing it. Don't stop.* "Then you know I won't give up," he said. "Let's negotiate."

The Deathweaver continues drawing. As it speaks, the orb inside its body sparkles with energy. "Based on our graphs, we have determined that our negotiations with you, while inadvisable, appear to be unpre-ventable." The Deathweaver pushes Axel away from its pad, more gently this time, and says, "Speak your piece, creature."

Axel struggles to make phrases meet in his mind. "Holy shit," he whispers then slams his jaw shut—terrified he might have wasted his moment on something frivolous.

The Deathweaver, once again, does not react. As its pen-wielding tentacles continue mapping the universe, and as its translucent skin reflects the cosmos that it is helping to craft, three of its heavy eyes spin to look at Axel. "Speak what you must speak," the Deathweaver says. "And we shall consider."

Axel clears his throat. *This is so weird.* "All right. Look. I get that you've got to keep reality... balanced, or whatever. People have to die so other things can happen. I get it." His chest tightens. It's hard to speak. He closes his eyes, counts to three, and then reopens them. "I'll give you anything, *anything*, so that Gwendolyn doesn't die this way. She's too young. The kid deserves to have a full life. I know you can't bring back Brooklyn, her mother, but please, tell me what I can trade so Gwen can live."

Axel hears vibrations from his other side, and when he turns, a different Deathweaver—one just as engaged in its drawings—is now speaking to him. "Are you aware how many youthful creatures perish in any given hour?" it says in a slightly different modulation from its partner. With a clear sense of irritation, the entity's massive head swerves over to one of its pads, returning to work. "It is an unfortunate part of the formula."

"The equations which rely on this child's termination are unalterable," the first Deathweaver says. "She must die today to maintain cosmic balance."

"Take my life in her place," Axel says.

The tentacled beast stops moving its pens for a moment. Several of its eyes narrow. Then it resumes. "Your life is not equal to hers. It is not enough."

Axel falls back. *Well, shit, that's harsh.* He struggles to not feel hopeless and focuses on the memory of Gwendolyn hugging her mother. *Her dead mom. Like she'll soon be dead. Keep talking, Axel.*

"Fair enough," he says. "What can I give up that will be equal? What can I do to... balance this out, so you won't kill this little girl? Because seriously—" He wipes away tears. "I won't pretend I have any goddamn idea what the hell you things are, what your life is, or if you're even alive. But I'll tell you, all of us tiny, stupid creatures in the living world, with no control over the universe, have to constantly suffer from the consequences of what you do. And I get it, you need to balance some celestial equation, or whatever. And I've been through a lot of your shitty balancing myself, I'll bet." He clenched his fists. *It's not personal. Nothing they do is personal. Don't blame them for Aaron and Shoshana.* He inhaled, exhaled, and kept going. "But I will do absolutely anything so that you can spare this wonderful, pure little kid. To give her another chance." He looked at one Deathweaver, then the other. "And until you give me an opportunity, a trade, something, I won't leave you alone. You'll have to kill me or wipe me out of reality, because I won't back down."

The two Deathweavers gaze directly at him for a long moment. The second one emits a soft chirping noise to yet another Deathweaver next to it, and they look at one another. Then, with shocking fierceness, the first two Deathweavers rip off the front pages of their sketchbooks. They whip their pens across, redrawing the formula, quickly filling their pages with a new set of geometric figures, equations, and arrows. They glance at one another's pad, comparing notes, and then continue.

Axel inches forward. "What's happening?"

The first Deathweaver pushes him back. "Wait."

Axel pushes his feet into the black sand, trying to box up his emotions before they burst out of him. He watches as the Deathweavers continue drawing new shapes. Then one of them stops for a moment, followed by the other. They both face Axel.

"There is one way," the second Deathweaver says. Its electrical voice singes the air. "Consider this a favor."

"Tell me," Axel cries out with naked desperation. "Anything."

"Two things must be traded in exchange for the child's life." The Deathweaver glances back at its sketchbooks, then eyes Axel. "First, as you are aware, a particularly odious faction of your species has created a hideous aberration in our land—"

"The Glass City." Axel nods. "But I don't count those Kindred assholes as being from the same species as me."

"Yes," the Deathweaver says while resuming its work. "To fulfill your obligations in a manner that allows us to redraw the pattern, you must go to this Glass City, and you must destroy it for us."

Axel's heart leaps with excitement. "Okay. Okay." He clasps his hands together. "How do I do that?"

"By first destroying the Glass City's protector. That is, the being you call the Stranger. It is, indeed, a fragile place. If the Stranger falls, so will the synthetic detritus from which it arose."

Axel stares out at the ocean for a moment, soaking in the reality of what is happening. Fear and excitement crash into each other, much like waves colliding with the shore. "So, I kill the Stranger, sure. But aren't there tons of Strangers, every time Kindred programs a new one into somebody else?"

"All of them run from the same program. If you end one, it shall end them all."

"But how do I, uh, kill it?"

"That is for you to determine. It will certainly try to stop you. The Stranger has, in fact, already located this Gwendolyn—the being you are trying to save—and is trying to pull her into its domain. Through enough trauma, it may succeed at severing many fragments of her being and trapping them here in the Deathscape, where they will be unable to scale the Great Tree. That is what it intends for you, as well."

Axel trembles. "Won't let that happen." *Can't let that happen. Even if I have to sacrifice my own happy eternity to that thing, I won't let it trap Gwen. I hope.*

"We shall see," the first Deathweaver says.

The second Deathweaver draws a long, curvy line along the bottom of its pad. "We can always rework the pattern back to its original shape if you fail. It is of little concern to us, but the elimination of the Glass City would be pleasant."

Axel shakes his head, trying not to think about the terrifying scenario that awaits him. "Okay, so I bust Kindred's colony. Take down the Stranger, with..." *How the hell do I do that? They won't say shit. Move on.* "Whatever. And if I do that, you'll spare Gwen?"

"Not quite." The third Deathweaver's pen draws a shape unlike anything Axel has ever seen, and its tone is the deepest of them all. "If you are successful at destroying the aberration, you will also need to make a sacrifice."

"Like what?"

"If the child does not join us here in the Deathscape today, as was planned..." The Deathweaver's electric voice tingles through Axel's ears. "Then it will necessitate that you give up the memory you love the most."

Axel frowns. "Huh. A memory?"

"Yes. The memory of the lake house, from your childhood. It must be wiped away from your mind. Forever."

Axel shudders at how casually the creature knows the inner contents of his mind, from his deepest fears to his most beloved recollections. He feels violated. *It does know. And it wants to take it away from me.* He thinks of himself as a little boy, standing out there with his parents, staring out into the water—much like the water he now stares into. *Mama told me to never forget that day. It's the one day that I can't lose. The only memory I have of them.* He notices, for the first time, that there are even more Deathweavers swimming beneath the waves, their tentacles working away at unseen machinery.

"You can't be serious," Axel whispers. "It's the only memory I have with my parents."

"Yes, and when you sacrifice it—" The first creature clicks and chirps again to the other creature beside it. "You will have no memories of them at all, other than the car crash in which they passed over to this realm. That is how balance will be maintained."

Rage fills Axel's heart. "How the fuck can my life not be worth Gwen's, but a single memory from my childhood is?"

"The Everything is complex and multifaceted," the Deathweaver says. "Every action, every moment, and every decision factors into an infinite number of other ones. The impact of that single memory, Axel Rivers, goes far beyond you, and it is written that, in its present form, it will alter the fates of countless others. If Gwendolyn comes back, and this memory remains in you, then everything—*everything*—will be thrown into chaos, for reasons far beyond your comprehension. The loss of that memory, then, will also cause severe alterations to the pattern of what must happen."

"But I don't matter."

"You are not inconsequential, creature." The Deathweaver's eyes glow. "You, and all living beings, are the fabric from which each universe and dimension are sewn together. We are the ones that sew it. Everything reverberates infinitely, forever, and if you do what we ask, we shall be able to balance the maps in such a way that the child may live and go forward to have a happy, fulfilling life. She will live long. She will be known as a notable musician and songwriter. She will marry when she is thirty-three years old. Have two of her own children. Or..." It pauses to examine its maps and then returns to work. "You can ignore our requests, and she will die today. The choice is yours."

Axel closes his eyes. He shakes with anger. *If I lose that memory, I lose them.* He forces himself to relive every detail of the beautiful night on the lake, all the images and scenes that he's held tightly onto over the years. *Mama. Papa. The chiminea. The music—Papa's guitar, Mama's singing, the song—she called it "Ending Forever."* He tries to break free from the nostalgia, but the voice of his mother rings in his ears, telling him, '*When you remember these moments, they last forever. You promise to remember this?*'

His shoulders slump. "There has to be another way."

"Listen carefully, Axel Rivers. If this girl is to live, then the Glass City must fall at your hands, and the memory of your parents must be lost. This conversation has reached its termination point. You may proceed as you wish."

Axel gazes upon the all-powerful being before him. He wants to argue. To fight. As far as he's come, though, he knows he has hit the very limits of what's possible in a universe that, despite its colossal size, still has clear boundaries. *There's only one path left.* He walks away from the Deathweavers in a daze. He strolls out into the cool waves, feeling them lap at his ankles, and watches the underwater Deathweavers swimming through the waves. *You know what you gotta do.*

He reaches down into the water, and as it courses through his fingers, he quietly says, "I'm sorry, Mama." He walks back to the Deathweavers. "I agree to the conditions. How do I get to the Glass City?"

Chapter 15: The Glass City

The Glass City rises high in the mountains of the Deathscape, fortressed by shimmering, mirrored walls. From far away, it seems mystical, like something from a fairy tale. Once close, though, this fantastical image gives way to cracks and dust. The transparent walls are bumpy and smudged with dirt. They don't align quite properly. Screws, rivets, and brackets hold fractured pieces together in a haphazard manner. Glowing blue signs for Kindred Eternal Solutions hang from the outer walls—a monument to advertising for the sake of advertising—with the lights for certain letters burnt out. One sign, in particular, is so neglected that it now reads "in red Eternal Sol."

The front doors of the Glass City are flanked by enormous, glittering stone statues of each of Kindred's wealthy founders. As Axel walks between them, the high-pitched whine of the city rings in his ears. He shakes his head in disgust. After hiking for hours—without the Stranger teleporting him there, the road proved quite long—he feels oddly disappointed by how spiritually empty this man-made construction feels. Staring at his reflection on the walls and the shimmering skyscrapers contained within, he is reminded of a slick-looking personal computer that a former friend showed off to him in the early 2000s, which was tricked out with all the buzziest modifications but ran unfunctionally slow.

The Glass City's pearly-white gates open for him, emitting a small, prerecorded jingle. Axel gazes back one last time at the majesty of the natural Deathscape—his eyes trace the highest branches of the Great

Tree as they stretch across the universe—then he crosses over into the corporate prison that beckons him.

The gates creak shut behind him. Instantly, the Glass City's horrible internal siren dials up to maximum volume, and it screams into his head. He bites down, hard, gripping his head on both sides. *Can't think. Focus. Feels like my skull is gonna split in two. Hang tight. Walk, walk.*

His eyes water. *Keep walking. Do it for Gwendolyn. Keep. Walking.* He stumbles out into the midst of the shimmering and empty metropolis, even as every muscle feels electrified by the cacophonous noise.

Finally, the whine subsides enough that he can think straight. Before he can take in his surroundings, he is interrupted by the crackle of overhead speakers. "Welcome to Kindred's Metropolis-1 base," calls out the same electronic female voice from the orientation video, so long ago. "Enjoy your stay in the afterlife. Feel free to sample the wondrous sights in the watchtower. Stop at the café to enjoy a drink. Enjoy a quick snack at..."

Axel leaves these announcements in the dust. He rounds the corner and steps into a public square, where he is surrounded by glowing blue Kindred signs. Here, he stops, lifts his arms to the sky, and he bellows, "Stranger!" He waits a moment. "I'm here for you!"

The Stranger does not appear. "Wimp," he mutters. After waiting for a moment, Axel continues walking. The crystallized streets crackle under his heels. Shimmering glass skyscrapers claw into the stars and galaxies above, trying to puncture their beauty. Whenever he approaches a physical structure, the horrible whine amplifies, as if touching anything will cause it to pierce him like a needle. *Better not come close to any of this Kindred stuff, then. Guess there's a mutual hatred.* He keeps waiting to see any signs of human presence, but the closest he can find is a storefront with cameras and a TV screen that plays a recording of him entering the city. *Seems like Metropolis-1 isn't open for business yet. I'm their first tourist. Lucky me.* He trudges between the buildings, peering through glass alleys and into glass houses. He sees empty swimming pools and empty hot tubs. Bars that haven't opened yet, and there are no beers being served. Storefronts are visible, with empty shelves but prices already listed. *All this shit. A whole new dimension and all these assholes can think to do is badly replicate what they have when they're alive instead of soaking up new things.*

The soft cry of a child runs through his heart like a knife. "Help me, Axel!"

Axel races down the street—between an empty casino and an empty museum—trying to figure out where the noise came from. "Gwen?" He sees nothing but more buildings, structures, and illuminated Kindred monuments.

"Help..." Her voice is fading.

Axel spins in a circle. "Gwen, I hear you!" He flips around, runs backward, and stumbles into a park, where yet another statue of Kevin Tyler, the world's first trillionaire, stands above a fountain of glowing turquoise water that has clearly been stolen from the rivers of the Deathscape. Axel races up and down the park as Gwendolyn's whimpering fades in and out. "Say something, Gwen!" He pants, out of breath. "Show me where you are—"

"I'm here," a frightened little voice says from above his head.

Axel looks up. His jaw drops. Gwendolyn is suspended over the park in a floating glass cage. Half of her body has dissolved into a fine, golden dust, and with her remaining arm, she desperately reaches down to Axel. "Please, Axel, I'm so scared."

"I'm here," Axel says. *Don't break down. Don't collapse. You're her only chance.* "I'll find a way."

"You will not," the Stranger answers.

The black robes of Kindred's living termination program descend from above, floating downward until the Stranger is only a few yards away from him. Its shadow reflects like a thunderstorm upon every mirrored surface of the city, from the streets to the skyscrapers. Axel tries to march forward, but his courage crumbles when the Stranger reopens its robes and reveals the child's skeleton buried in its muddy chest. Flowers and mushrooms sprout from the remains.

"You're full of shit," Axel says, but his voice is shaking. *It's not human. It's not Aaron. Just a program designed to control you. You have to kill it. Somehow.* However, the Stranger's mask—still split in half, between the faces of Gwendolyn and Aaron—twists back into a loathsome plastic smirk, on both visages, and Axel becomes paralyzed.

"You have failed at everything in your life. You were meant to fail," the Stranger's voice crackles. "And you will fail again."

Fear strikes Axel's heart. "Maybe. But I can't let you win this." He's shaking. He knows that the Stranger isn't falling for his bravado. *It's not wrong. I have failed at everything. How the hell could I succeed this time?*

"You cannot," the Stranger says, responding to his thoughts. The plastic smiles on its masks widen further, to the point of looking crocodilian. "You mean nothing to the universe. Even in your world, you are nothing. A statistic. A burden on taxpayers. An orphan with no place in the world. Not in life. Not in death. No past. No future."

The Stranger lunges forward. Its bloody, mangled hand seizes Axel's face. Its cold, wet palm smothers Axel's mouth. He screams as it digs its gnarled fingernails into his cheeks, chin, and temples. He hears a series of small pops as his facial skin breaks in the Stranger's grip, and his skull starts to crack. *No no no can't be like this, stay awake, don't let it, don't...*

His vision goes dark.

"Axel?" He hears Dr. Carpenter say. *"Are you waking up?"*

He roars in anger and pain. Tears roll down his cheeks. *Losing again. Like I always lose. Like I've lost everything. Like I lost Aaron.* Light flickers back into his eyes, and the Stranger's dual masks loom before him. His head feels like a balloon about to explode.

"Axel, again, are you waking up?" Dr. Carpenter cries out from the living world.

"No!" Axel rips his head out of the Stranger's grasp, flinging himself backward into a glass wall. The entire structure shatters, and he is sprawled out on the ground, surrounded by its shards. *Glass. Breaks easily.* He jumps back to his feet. He glares at the Stranger. *Guilt. Fear. This fucking thing was made to break me. A manipulation. If I remember that... if I REMEMBER what it's doing...*

He gazes at another glass wall beside him, already half broken. He smashes his fist against it, and it shatters, leaving bleeding cuts all over his hand. He smirks. *Fragile.* He rubs his wounds. "Glass is fragile," he mutters. He faces the Stranger. "I'm not."

The Stranger creeps toward him. Gwendolyn cries above. Axel trembles with fear, but he focuses on his feet on the ground, his shoulders held high, and he marches ahead—right toward the creature that terrifies him. "Who I am, what I do..." he says. "All of it matters. Every action is part of what forms the universe. That's what the Deathweavers said."

The Stranger's dark robes flutter in the wind. Axel smashes his foot against the ground. The street fractures into tiny pieces.

"Okay. Yeah." He pushes forward, feeling the Stranger's unexpected nervousness flow into him. "Maybe the world doesn't give a shit about me. Maybe I got a raw deal and have made shitty decisions. But I matter. That girl —" He points at Gwendolyn. "She matters. Like her mom did. And unlike you, asshole, I'm not fragile."

The Stranger lunges forward again, emitting an unearthly shriek that sends Axel reeling. *Focus, don't run.* The entity's hands clutch his throat. Axel can't breathe. *Remember, it's fragile. If you don't let it break through you, it can't stand on its own.* He grabs the Stranger's shoulders and throws it to the ground. He leaps atop it and lets loose with a spree of punches. Suddenly, its black robes stiffen. Its body cracks. As Axel hits the Stranger over and over again, its form breaks into smaller and smaller shards of black glass.

Axel stands up, panting. Sweat pours down his back. His knuckles are torn to shreds. Below him, the Stranger's pieces start to move back together and reform. "Ah, shit," Axel says. *It just comes back together if it breaks. What the hell do I do?*

He gets ready to pummel the entity again, but from the glass cage above, Gwendolyn cries out. "Axel, its mask!"

Smart kid. Axel climbs atop the Stranger, pins it down, and grabs its double-faced mask. It claws at him in desperation. Axel yanks at both sides of the mask, splitting it fully down the middle, then rips each half free.

There is no face behind the mask.

Nothing.

Nothing at all. Just empty darkness. The Stranger groans, clawing away from him, but it is fading—fading into a dark mist, a nothingness. Axel drops the pieces of its mask behind him—and as these remains clatter to the ground, the earth rumbles.

"Gwen." Axel calls out. A crack rips through the ground, spitting rocks into the sky. "Can you—"

The trillionaire statue explodes into fragments. At the edge of the city, an empty glass skyscraper comes tumbling down, spewing fractalized shards. Gwendolyn's cage shatters, and as she tumbles downward, Axel leaps up just in time to catch her. He folds her within his arms in midair and tumbles back to the ground, skinning his knees.

"Axel!" she cries.

"I've got you!" He pushes her underneath him, blocking her from the explosions of glass happening all around them. Shards rip open his flesh. He screams at the pain. Jagged pieces embed themselves deep in his skin. Buildings collapse. Bridges blow apart. The Glass City tumbles down.

And suddenly, he can't feel anything. Not the glass. Not his body. He feels himself transform into a gentle mist, carried away in the wind, deep into the Deathscape, as everything that remains of the Glass City destroys itself. He can't speak. He can't see. Everything is gold. *Where am I?* he thinks. *Is Gwendolyn...?"*

"She's okay," Shoshana whispers in his ear. "But there's something else you still need to do."

AXEL WAKES UP AT THE lake house, from his favorite childhood memory. This time, though, he is an adult. His body is no longer torn to pieces, but it is covered in scars—thick, puffy ones, that will never go away. He shakes his head, feeling dizzy, uncertain whether he is in the Deathscape, a dream, or the waking world.

"Gwendolyn..." He stops. *Shoshana said she's safe. She's safe. I hope. But why am I here?* "Hello?"

The night air is warm. The porch creaks beneath his steps. The smell of a cookout flows into his nostrils. On the other side of the chiminea is his childhood self, now a separate being. *It's not me anymore. It's someone else who used to have my body.* When he tries to call out to the boy, his voice is silent, and he realizes that he has become an observer in his memory rather than a participant.

He breathes in the water, the wind, and the warmth of the fire. *This feels more real than it ever did in my memory. Like I'm really there again.* Glowing sparks fly out of the chiminea. The boy cuddles up to his mama, and she sings to him. Papa is leaning against the rail on one arm, grinning as he watches.

The little boy says to his mother, "I don't want this day to end. It's been the best day ever."

Mama smiles. "It will end," she says. And the adult Axel, hearing the words he has replayed in his head over and over throughout the decades since she died, mouths her response alongside her. "Everything does."

Axel looks away. *Gwendolyn. The Glass City. I must've broken it. I must be...* He looks around him, trying to spot the Great Tree, but all he can see is the memory he is reliving. He realizes, guiltily, that much of the conversation between his childhood self and his mother has passed by him, and he turns to face it again.

"Now look at the stars," Mama says. "Look at how many of them there are. Space—it's so enormous, isn't it? And say —"

"I will remember that."

"You won't remember, though." Mama turns and faces Axel—the real, adult Axel, not the memory. "Because you made a promise to the Deathweavers, and all of this is gone."

Axel jumps. *She's staring right at me. Mama.* Tears well up in his eyes. "I'm sorry. I had to."

Mama smiles. "You did have to. You saved that little girl's life. And I'm so proud of you." She steps forward and hugs Axel tightly. Before he can process this, the hug grows tighter, as Papa joins with them. He melts into their embrace, breaking down in tears, feeling the parental love that, throughout all these years, has been almost forgotten. Both his parents clutch him tightly.

He looks at them again. Their hair has grayed. Their skin has wrinkled. Both of them are elderly now, as they would be today if the car crash never occurred. Choking back a sob and hugging them again, Axel says, "I'm sorry. I don't want to forget. I don't... Mama, Papa, I don't..."

"But you must, Ax," Papa says, kissing his cheek. "And you will. But somewhere, deep inside, we will always be with you. The love we gave to you... it will live on inside you."

"Even if you don't know where it came from," Mama adds.

They pull away from him. Axel tries to hug them again, but they are out of reach. And then the two people before him—the mightiest beings in his universe, the ones he has fought so hard to keep alive despite their being dead for so long—have no faces. They are blank. Expressionless. He blinks back more tears, and their bodies twist away into nothingness, until he barely knows who they are. *I had parents.* He tries to place them. *Why can't I remember my parents? What did they look like? Their voices... what did they sound like?* When he says their names in his mind, the only image he draws is of a broken, bleeding car windshield. "Where did I come from?" He whispers.

Sadness overwhelms him. He doesn't remember.

AFTER WHAT FEELS LIKE an eternity, Axel finds himself standing in a pool of water between two giant roots of the Great Tree, staring up at the mystical colossus before him. The tree's billions of branches move and sway through the universe. Its roots breathe in and out. It is linked to everything that exists. He looks down at his feet. Tiny, feeble roots spring from the mud, and touch his ankles.

His mind is blank. He can't remember what just happened to him. *I was there in the Glass City... but then? What happened?* His eyes are damp. *I lost something.* The harder he strains to remember it, the deeper it pockets itself. Soon, every trace of it is gone, and despite the grandeur that surrounds him, he feels awful. A strange, nagging *something* is gone. A something that mattered to him. A something that he knows he can never have again.

Then, to Axel's cosmic humiliation, he breaks down crying at the foot of the universe itself. Tears streak down his face. He crouches in the water and sobs like he hasn't done since he was a child first hearing, in a cold hospital waiting room, that his parents were dead. *I don't know what to do.* Panic races down his spine. Despair clenches his heart. *I lost something. What was it? What the hell was it?* He crawls to the shore, digs his fingers into the bark of the giant root, and then collapses into it.

He lays there. *It's gone.*

Warmth passes over him like the sun. Lips kiss his forehead, and the voice of his son says, "I love you, Daddy."

Axel trembles. "Aaron?"

"I just want you to know I'm doing great," Aaron says. "You stay strong out there."

Then, as Axel tries to get up, Shoshana speaks, as well. "And don't worry if you get sad sometimes, while you're there on Earth," she says. "Because sadness is part of what makes you *alive*. Sadness is human. And don't be afraid to find some happiness, either, because that's part of being human, too. It's all interconnected. It's all part of *you*."

"We're with you, Daddy," Aaron says, "Always. And you're with us, too."

Axel finally gathers the strength to climb to his feet, desperately hoping that he'll see their faces. All that greets him is a golden mist, which soon fades. The glowing white tendrils of many flowers, sprouting from the roots, are winding around him. The sky throbs with pulsating energy. When he gazes up at the highest branches of the Great Tree, he hears a gentle laughing sound—and he recognizes it as belonging to Aaron and Shoshana, together. Millions upon millions of sparks of light, grown from the good deeds of their lives, soaring through the universe and reconnecting with everything that ever existed, or will exist. They are part of the Everything, and that means they are a part of him, too. Even now, after dying three times, he can scarcely imagine.

He holds out his hand. Shimmers of light dance across the palm. Lives, souls, pieces of those he loves, living eternally in all that they loved. *One thing I do know is that death isn't the end.* Shoshana had been right, all those years ago, on the night they'd first met. Just as he'd been right when he once told Aaron that the water in a puddle never dies—it just changes. *Energy cannot be created or destroyed. We don't disappear. We don't go away. We just change into something else, and maybe... maybe...*

"Maybe that's okay." He smiles. He stares up into the endless branches of the Great Tree, wondering which ones his energies will someday dance along. "I'll meet you guys up there someday." He shrugs. "But not yet."

He lies down on the mud beside the turquoise water, his back nestled into one of the great roots. It feels warm and comforting to be there, as if the root was perfectly molded for his body. He closes his eyes—stealing one last look at the glories of the Deathscape—and then everything goes dark. The smells and sounds dissipate. Axel feels his son and wife slipping through his fingers as the physical world reforms around him, but he isn't afraid to be alive again. Not anymore.

There is a sharp pinch in his arm.

THE SUN GLARED INTO Axel's eyes as he resurrected for the last time. Its rays pierced through the bay window, revealing giant particle clouds of dust spinning through the air in a fashion that, when Axel was young, he'd often thought looked magical. He stirred. *Where am I? I can't remember.* His muscles ached. He timidly touched the skin of his forearm, and a slew of protruding scars from the Glass City—fully healed but also fully present—made themselves known, answering any lingering questions he had about whether injuries in the Deathscape became injuries in real life, as well.

A needle slid out of his vein, and he jumped. "Ouch!"

"Welcome back to the land of the living." Dr. Kendra Carpenter smiled at him, though her pleasantries no longer brought much comfort. "How did it go? I'll admit, I thought I lost you there. Your readings went dead cold, if you'll pardon the pun. Must've been an equipment error, since we're not in the lab, and... hey." The doctor's eyes crinkled. "What're you smiling about?"

Axel hadn't realized he was smiling, but when he touched his face, he couldn't deny it. "Huh." His lips stretched wider, as if he were being tickled. "Don't know. Just feels good to be back."

"Alrighty then." The doctor took his pulse. Axel grinned at the booming heart in his wrist. When she was done, he sat upright, uncomfortably remembering that he was lying on the woman's bed. *She must've slept on her couch. If she even slept. Probably didn't.* Sensory details seemed almost unbearably vivid. When he glanced at the cluttered bedside table, the title of every book looked back at him simultaneously. The fabric of Dr. Carpenter's slacks glistened with complexity. The smell of dust overpowered his nostrils, and there was a hint of hot wax from a candle she must have lit the night before. *Heh. Almost feels like I'm stoned. Weird.* He sat upright, slowly piecing the living world together again.

Suddenly, reality hit him like a splash of ice water to the face. *Gwen.* "Did it work?" He stood up, wavering on his feet. "Is she alive?"

"Axel, I don't even know the girl you were trying to save. I forgot her name, frankly, if you even told me." Dr. Carpenter shrugged. "Did it work in the Deathscape? There's your answer, and that's what I want to know. You owe me the full story."

"I think it worked. I just need to —" His phone rang. It was Cindy. He looked at Dr. Carpenter for a moment, then swung the phone to his ear. "How is she?" He heard sobbing. *Oh, fuck.* "Cindy," he said, his voice rattling. *If she's dead, it was all for nothing. But no, I gave up... something. Something big. She has to be alive.* "How is Gwen?"

"Axel." Cindy exhaled. "I don't know how it happened. It just —"

"Is she..." He couldn't finish the sentence.

"She's going to be okay!" Cindy laughed, and Axel realized that her tears came from happiness, not grief. "It's gotta be a miracle, Axel, if you believe in that sort of thing. She's going to be okay. And when she woke up, she said... said..." Cindy cleared her throat. "She said 'Thank you, Axel,' that's what she said. I don't get what she meant. I haven't been able to ask her. But if you did something... hell, I don't know what you could've done, when you were running around last night. Did you, though? How?"

Axel smiled so hard that his cheeks hurt. "Nah, didn't do anything." He closed his eyes, held his chest, and his heart felt good. "Nothing at all."

Chapter 16: Ending the Beginning

The living room of Axel's apartment had become a maze of cardboard boxes, most of them packed to the gills. He'd lifted the furniture downstairs into the moving truck hours ago. The holes in the walls had been spackled. The TV, toaster, and other appliances were packed up. Axel struggled to remember what the apartment had looked like only a few days ago, but its new appearance had already wiped away the past. That was okay by him. He was ready to move on.

It feels good to be doing this. Real good. That was the strange thing. When he'd first heard that Malik and his boyfriend were moving in together, he'd been happy for them. However, when they'd asked Axel to join them as a roommate, he'd greeted the offer with disbelief.

"No, we're serious," Malik had said. *"It's a big place, and it'd be a big help with our rent. There's a totally separate room on the second floor, even has its own bathroom, and if you don't take it, I'm just gonna find some college kid or something, anyway. And hey, it'll give you a chance to move on. Stay with us as long as you want. You've gotta leave that old place behind, man."*

Malik was right, as usual. Axel knew that. And as soon as he'd agreed to move in—on a date that was, bizarrely, exactly six months from the night he'd died in Dr. Carpenter's apartment—it was as if more bricks kept perfectly falling into place. Right after that, he'd found a decent-paying new job. After that, he'd gotten word that, following Kindred's recent legal struggles, all the former test subjects like him would be receiving settlements. His payout, in fact, was big enough to finally pay off his debt. So much had happened—so much had changed—that Axel could still barely process it, but he had a gut feeling that so long as he kept walking forward, the proper road would appear before him.

And that's why I'm here. To move on. So let's finish this. Axel passed through the kitchen, checking whether he'd missed anything. *Looks clean.* He ran his fingers down the counter and remembered the many times that the little toddler version of Aaron had clutched that counter with his pudgy toddler hands, trying to grab whatever was on it, usually with a beaming, mischievous toddler smile. It had taken hours of trial-and-error to find the right babyproofing system to keep the kid from getting all the pots and pans out of the cabinets below. Axel smiled to himself. *Hey, Aaron. Miss you. Always will.*

He walked down the hallway to face off against the last two rooms that hadn't been packed up—his bedroom, and Aaron's room. Axel stared at both closed doors, feeling overwhelmed. *You can do this.* He breathed in heavily. *If you can die three times and come back, you can clean out your damn apartment.*

Behind him, the front door popped open, and Malik came in, lugging two massive armfuls of folded boxes. He dumped them onto the hallway floor. "All right, dude." He panted. "Living room looks all packed up. Are these rooms...?"

"Nah." Axel shook his head. "It's not a... uh..." he started then clammed up. *No, put it out there. Be honest with your best friend. Honesty brings healing.* "I tried, but it was hard. Haven't even opened these doors," he said finally. "So many emotions tied up in this stuff. Some of it will be easier if you just—"

"Got it." Malik squeezed Axel's shoulder and clapped him on the back. "We should split up. Each pack up a room. You want me to take Aaron's room, maybe?"

"Yeah." Axel sighed relievedly. "Thanks."

"No problem," Malik said, disappearing into the room with a load of folded boxes. From inside, he called out, "Just let me know whatever you need, okay? Love you, man. Can't believe we're finally gonna be roomies!"

"Thanks," Axel repeated. And with that, he summoned up his courage to carry his own pile of boxes into his and Shoshana's bedroom.

Immediately, the sights and smells of the room—which he hadn't seen in weeks—were a gut-punch. *Keep going.* Piles of Shoshana's items were everywhere. Clothes. Jewelry. Notebooks. *It's insane that I just left it all sitting here so long.* He swallowed. *Or maybe it's not insane. Maybe it's just because I loved her so much, wanted her to come back, and if I moved her stuff...* He shook his head. *Keep going.* He folded together one box, taped it, and labeled it "DONATE." And in that box, he started putting away her clothes. Socks, pants, items that he hadn't seen since she was alive, all of it went into the box. However, one scarf carried a whiff of her scent, and Axel had to step away. The memories this scarf had released weighed too heavily on him.

Go to the dresser. Do something else. But keep moving.

The dresser wasn't much easier. Beneath another pile of her jewelry, pens, and hair ties, he spotted the same folded-up note that he'd first seen there, so long ago, when he was still involved with Kindred. Written on the top of it was his name. With trembling hands, he picked up the note, unfolded it, and—without even reading the text—admired the gentle swoops and angles of her handwriting as if he were hearing her voice again. He pressed the paper to his chest. "I love you," he whispered. "I'll read it."

He read it.

Dear Axel...

As I write this, my love, the tickets to Florida are already purchased. You're as quiet and broody as ever, but I know what you're feeling, perhaps more than you know. You feel like this is the end. You feel like a widening gulf has formed between us and that we can no longer go back to who we were before. You feel like your inability to communicate clearly to me has made it impossible to function. You think our relationship is on the verge of collapse.

Well, mister, you're wrong.

Yes, Axel, I'm frustrated. I'm angry. Too often, I feel like you don't care, and I need more from you. I'm 100 percent sick of the way that you just get quiet and won't talk for days when something upsets you. But I knew who you were when I met you. I knew it when we shared that beautiful sunset on the top of the hill. And I knew it when I married you. When I NEED you, even in the darkest moments, you have ALWAYS been there. Yes, you're emotionally unavailable, but relationships are co-constructed, and focusing on your flaws, the way you always do, ignores the fact that I've got my own problems, and those are part of our dynamic, too. I'm micromanaging, petty, too analytic... and for all my focus on talking about problems, I ALSO clam up and apologize instead of speaking clearly. For God's sake, Axel, I'm writing this partly because I'm too afraid to say it aloud. You always paint this idealized picture of me, and it's frustrating, because I'm just as messy as you are.

I'm complaining. I'm sorry (there I go again!). My point is, Axel, we might have some issues to work out, but I fucking love, love, love, love you. I will always love, love, love you. You're the man I always dreamed of finding. The most devoted and loving father I've ever seen. A deep, sensitive soul who has been damaged by the world but does everything he can to love and protect those he cares for. I love you, Axel. I want you to come to Florida with me, but if you don't, we'll work things out when I get back: I know it, deep down, even though it's so painful for me to go away from you that I can barely handle it. We WILL make this work. We WILL be together, forever, and I promise you that no matter what, I'll always love you. Call me when you read this.

Love,
Your "Shosh"

P.S. You remember that song you used to sing to Aaron to put him to sleep? The one about endings, eternity, legacies, all that, which you don't know the lyrics to, because they were in Khmer? The past few months, whenever you've been working late, I've been humming it to him after I read him a book at night. It really makes him feel happy, calm. He says it reminds him of you, so I'll hum it to him every night you're not there. He loves and admires you so much. Okay, footnote over.

Axel smiled to himself, clutching the note so tightly that he almost tore it. Weight spilled off his shoulders. *We would've been okay, I think. That's amazing to know.* Despite the sadness that would never fade, despite the loss that had scarred him, this realization made him feel better in a way he never could have realized.

"Hey," Malik said, leaning in the doorway. "You doing all right in there?"

Axel smiled. "Yeah, guess so. Hey, Malik, I've got a question for you. You remember if there was a special song I used to sing to Aaron? Can't remember it. I mean, I remember singing something, but I've got no idea what it was."

Malik glanced upward, thinking. "Huh. Actually, that sounds familiar."

"It does, right?"

"Yeah. Yeah. I remember you talking about it. It was in a different language, right? But we didn't know the words, or they weren't written down, or whatever. I think we even played an instrumental version of it with the band a few times. Way back." Malik scratched the back of his head.

Axel's phone vibrated. It was Cindy. "Hold on." He looked at Malik apologetically, and then answered it. "Hey," he said.

"Hey, Axel," Cindy replied. "You still coming over tonight? You-know-who has been excited about getting her guitar lesson all week —"

Axel chuckled. "Yeah, gotcha. Gotta do some packing through the afternoon, but nothing could ever stop me from being there. Same time as usual."

THE LIGHT DIMMED AS Axel drove down forested back roads. Until recently, he'd always hated this hour of the day—the dying hour, as he'd once called it. After his time with Kindred, though, twilight felt different to him, just as death felt different. The truth was that when the sun set, nothing truly ended, and nothing died. One day's death merely opened the door for a new day to begin. No matter what, everything kept spinning.

Driving again felt good. Even though his new car was the junkiest beater he'd ever driven, he loved the roaring engine, the steering wheel in his hands, and the freedom it offered. He still didn't drive much, but when he did, it was often to take the hour-long trip to the little apartment that Cindy, Naomi, and now Gwendolyn called home. The only part of the drive he didn't like was when he went over the bridge and passed by Sunrise Circle, the wealthy neighborhood that had all the beautiful lake houses. Every time he peered down that road and spotted the waterfront, chills went down his spine. He couldn't pinpoint why, exactly, these lake houses bothered him—the water itself was gorgeous. So was the architecture, and the trees. What made his aversion even weirder is that he knew, for a fact, that he'd used to take Aaron through Sunrise Circle, years ago, and they'd genuinely loved looking at those houses.

Not anymore. Now, something about the whole area made him feel deeply, miserably sad. He didn't know why.

Noticing that it was 5:30 p.m., Axel gently turned on the knob of the radio, where the newscaster was reciting the latest headlines. Axel drove for a while, half listening to updates from overseas, the economy, and so on, until a certain word—Kindred—caught him off guard. He turned up the volume.

"—another strange development, indeed," the newscaster said. "The stocks for Kindred Eternal Solutions have continued plummeting this morning, as they've done ever since their patented 'resurrection' technology was deemed an expensive failure. The lawsuits have only grown in scope and..."

Axel smirked. *Gotta wonder if me breaking down their Glass City has something to do with their issues. Nice to think that maybe it does. Maybe.* Ever since his third death, Kindred's business had gone down the tubes, with thousands of lawsuits, fines, and widespread allegations that their technology didn't work. It did work, of course, but Axel liked that the world thought it didn't. Even though he felt there'd probably be another Kindred someday—perhaps another attempt to colonize the Deathscape, maybe even with Dr. Carpenter involved—it was nice to know that the first effort had died off so unglamorously.

The radio announcer said the name Kevin Tyler, and Axel listened again. "Occurred when Tyler, the world's first trillionaire, was found dead this morning. The cause was ruled an overdose. Tyler was forty-one years old and was found by..."

Axel rubbed his chin. Death had once carried a strange and disturbing mystique, but now, whenever someone died, it felt different. *The Deathweavers decided it was his time,* he mused. *Ironic. The guy who wanted to live forever is gone now. Wonder if they found it amusing. If they get amused by anything.*

Axel pulled into the parking lot of the Turquoise Drive apartment complex. Three parallel brick buildings stood there, facing each other, each one crammed full of as many apartments as possible. It wasn't the nicest place, but Axel was glad that Gwendolyn had been able to stay with family. *Even if she doesn't get to grow up with her mother.* He sighed, pulled into the same spot he always did, and sat for a moment in the late-afternoon shadows. He checked his phone for missed calls and texts. Sure enough, Malik had texted him a picture of a sheet of paper with guitar chords on it. *Huh.* Underneath the photo, Malik had texted the message:

"Found this in one of your boxes. Pretty sure this is the song you were asking about, right?"

Axel's heart pounded. He felt a sudden pang of terror—as if just looking at the song for too long would rip open the scars of his past depression—and he pocketed his phone. Then, slowly, he lifted it back up, and he read the chords. They were completely unfamiliar. *So weird. But something about them is so... it hits me hard. Why?* He read them again, and hummed the song aloud. The tune rang deeply within him, but he didn't recognize it.

He grabbed his acoustic guitar from the backseat, got out of the car, and walked up to the apartment. He rang the doorbell, and Cindy opened the door.

"Hey, took you a long time to get here," Cindy said but with a smile. "Someone's been asking over and over again when you were going to —"

A shriek of excitement echoed across the apartment—"Axel!"—and the little girl who had so unexpectedly changed the course of Axel's life bounded over. He bent down right as Gwendolyn leapt into his arms, and she squeezed him so tight that, for a moment, it was as if nothing had ever gone wrong—as if Axel had never lost his family, as if Gwendolyn had never lost a mother. He cupped the back of her tiny head, holding her close.

"Hey, kid," he whispered, smiling. "Good to see you."

She pulled back, grinning with all her teeth. "I've missed you, Axel," she said. "Can we play guitar again, please? Show me how to do it?"

"Sure. That's why I'm here." Axel stared into her eyes, and he ran his thumb down the scar on her chin, one of the many marks the car crash had left her with—scars that eerily mirrored the ones the Glass City had left on him. She wasn't quite the same innocent girl he'd met on that one night when he'd walked her mother home, but the connection he and Gwendolyn had kept since then had, for him, been a tether through many dark storms.

"Let's go!" she said. "I love it when you make music."

Axel chuckled. "All right."

She took his hand and walked him to the living room, to the same spot where they always did guitar lessons. Axel slung the guitar off his shoulder, held it, took a deep breath, and a small voice inside him—a voice that he wanted to ignore but couldn't push aside—reminded him of Malik's text. *Play the song. The one he sent you.*

"So." Axel sat on the couch, as Gwendolyn sat across from him. "You want to show me what you've practiced?"

"Can you play something first?" she asked. "Something different, that I've never heard before. Not one of the usual songs on the radio."

Axel twitched. *Sometimes, I swear this kid is psychic.* His grip on the guitar loosened. "Why are you asking for that?"

"I don't know." She shrugged. "Can you? Please?"

Axel stared at her. *Play the song. When life is trying to tell you something, listen to it. You never know if it's some galactic octopus in the afterlife drawing out your path.* He glanced back at Cindy, who smiled at him from the kitchen, as she sipped on a glass of water. "Something different," he muttered. He put the guitar on his lap. Cold sweat trickled down his neck. *Play it.* "You sure?"

"Yes."

He got the guitar ready. Gwendolyn sat with him, gleefully fidgeting as she awaited his next move. *Play it.* Axel took out his phone and stared at the picture from Malik. He recited the music under his breath. *Malik would tell you to play it,* he thought. *Shoshana would, too. And Aaron...* Axel closed his eyes. *That's it. This was a song he loved, apparently. Gotta keep it alive, if just for that.*

"Are you okay, Axel?" Gwendolyn asked.

"Yeah." He wiped his brow. "Listen, Gwen—I told you about my son, Aaron."

"Yeah." She looked sad. "He died. Like Mommy did. Wish I could've met him."

Axel hung his head low. "Yeah." He looked up. "There was a song I used to sing to him. I don't know the words. Don't remember the song, honestly. Don't know why I sang it, if I'm being honest. But a friend of mine just found the chords again earlier today, and now it's hard to think of anything else. I'd like to play it. If that's okay with you."

"Yes! Please?"

Axel smiled, always elated by her enthusiasm for the littlest things. "Okay, will do." He took a deep breath, started practicing the opening notes, and to his shock, his fingers started playing ahead of him, as if the song that had left his mind was nonetheless still a part of his body. *Whoa. It feels really good to play this.* He kept practicing, and the tune—an ethereal, soft, slow, beautiful tune that cut deep into his heart and brought out feelings of warmth, comfort, and serenity that he'd forgotten about—flooded into every fiber of his being.

He missed a note. He stopped, embarrassed. Gwendolyn hugged him. "Keep playing," she said. "Please?"

"Okay," Axel said. Tears wet his eyes, and he began to play again, from the beginning. This time, he didn't slip. This time, every note rang through every muscle of his body, and his life seemed to play out in front of his eyes. As he played the song, somehow, he saw flashes of his favorite times with Shoshana—the night they'd met, the sunset on the top of the hill, the many nights they'd shared dinner together, the day Aaron was born—and he relived it all, in vivid color, as every ending birthed a new beginning. Throughout the entire song, Gwendolyn clung to him, giving him the closeness and comfort that she needed as much as he did.

Finally, Axel let the song draw to a close. He wiped his eyes. "Can you play it again?" Gwendolyn asked.

Axel laughed. "It's kinda heavy for me to play it, kid."

"But I love it." She pushed his hands back onto his guitar. "I don't want your song to ever, ever end."

"It'll end, one way or another," Axel said. "Everything does."

"I don't want it to," she said.

Axel stared into her eyes, and he knew that no matter how hard he tried to avoid it, the stubborn kid would eventually force him to play it again. He laughed. "Okay," he said. As he touched the strings of his guitar, her eyes lit up in response. He started playing, then stopped. "Tell you what," he said. "I'll play it one more time, but there's a lesson to learn here, too."

"What?"

"Well, basically, there's one way to make something last forever. Trick I've done throughout life. Don't know where I learned it, but it's helped me keep memories that I might've lost otherwise. Want to hear it?"

"Yeah!" she said. "I love tricks. And memories, too."

"All right." Axel lowered his guitar, and he pointed out the window. "Look at the sky. See the way the clouds are moving? Focus on them. Focus real intently, okay? Take in all the little details."

She stared carefully. "Okay."

"While you're focusing, okay, take a mental photo. You know what I mean? And say, 'I will remember this,' and you'll remember it."

"I will remember this."

"There you go." Axel placed her fingers on the strings of the guitar. "Now, think about what this guitar feels like in your hands. Think of the strings. The wood. The sound the guitar makes when you touch it. And then say the words, again."

"I will remember this," she giggled.

Axel laughed with her. "And as I play this song, focus real intently again, listen to every note, and say—"

"I will remember this!"

"Awesome." Axel grinned, and as he played her the song again, he said, "I'll remember this too."

Acknowledgments

There's a moment early in *Ending Forever* where Axel and Shoshana connect on their mutual status as "adult orphans." That's a label that also describes me. Honestly, becoming an adult orphan is probably what subconsciously drove me to finally write this book, after tinkering with some of the ideas for years beforehand. My father died when I was a teenager, and my mother died this past year: much of the raw grief that I experienced, in the wake of her passing, was funneled directly into this story. In fact, the flashback scene from the lake house, where Axel's mother teaches him how to save a moment, directly echoes a conversation I had with my own mother when I was a child. Thanks to her, and her lesson about how to remember things—"taking a mental snapshot," as she said—my own memories of the past remain as vivid as ever.

I write of my parents, here, not to focus on their absence, but instead, to acknowledge the profound impact that their guiding, nurturing love, and support has had on my life. I still feel them—both of them, each occupying their own unique space—in everything I do today. They truly were the best parents I could have asked for, and for as long as they *were* here, they gave everything they had to their children. I will never stop feeling grateful for that.

In the same vein, I also want to acknowledge my siblings, who faced the same loss I went through, each in their own ways. Because we have each other, and the ties that bind us, we will never truly be alone, and that support means more and more with every passing year.

Going through these past few years, between a pandemic and political turmoil, has been hard on everyone in the world, in ways both macro and micro. Through it all, my anchor to reality has been my wife, Veronica, who brings pure, unfiltered happiness to my heart just as much—if not even more—as she did when we first met. And as my wife has continued to lift my spirits and support my ambitions, I must also acknowledge the bubbly joy and positive energy of my daughter, Zaharina, who has made every part of life feel fuller, deeper, and more important.

I want to acknowledge my extended family and friends, who have never stopped dreaming my dreams alongside me. Gratitude also goes toward everyone who has talked to me about the concepts I deal with in this book, as well as the whole Red Adept Publishing team, particularly Lynn McNamee and my editor, Kim Husband, for continuing to support my strange, surreal fiction that doesn't easily fit into any specific genre box.

Given that this is a book about death, whatever comes after, and the impacts of our lives and decisions upon the wider universe, I'll finish by once again acknowledging all my other loved ones who have died in the past: Thank you for everything, and if you're reading this from somewhere else—wherever that "somewhere else" may be—then know how much I appreciate the time we did have, and how much your lives and essences will reverberate in everything I ever write. Thank you.

About the Author

Originally from California, Nicholas Conley has currently made his home in the colder temperatures of New Hampshire. He considers himself to be a uniquely alien creature with mysterious literary ambitions, a passion for fiction, and a whole slew of terrific stories he'd like to share with others.

When not busy writing, Nicholas is an obsessive reader, a truth seeker, a sarcastic idealist, a traveler, and — like many writers — a coffee addict.

Read more at www.nicholasconley.com/main/.

About the Publisher

Dear Reader,

We hope you enjoyed this book. Please consider leaving a review on your favorite book site.

Visit https://RedAdeptPublishing.com to see our entire catalogue.

Don't forget to subscribe to our monthly newsletter to be notified of future releases and special sales.